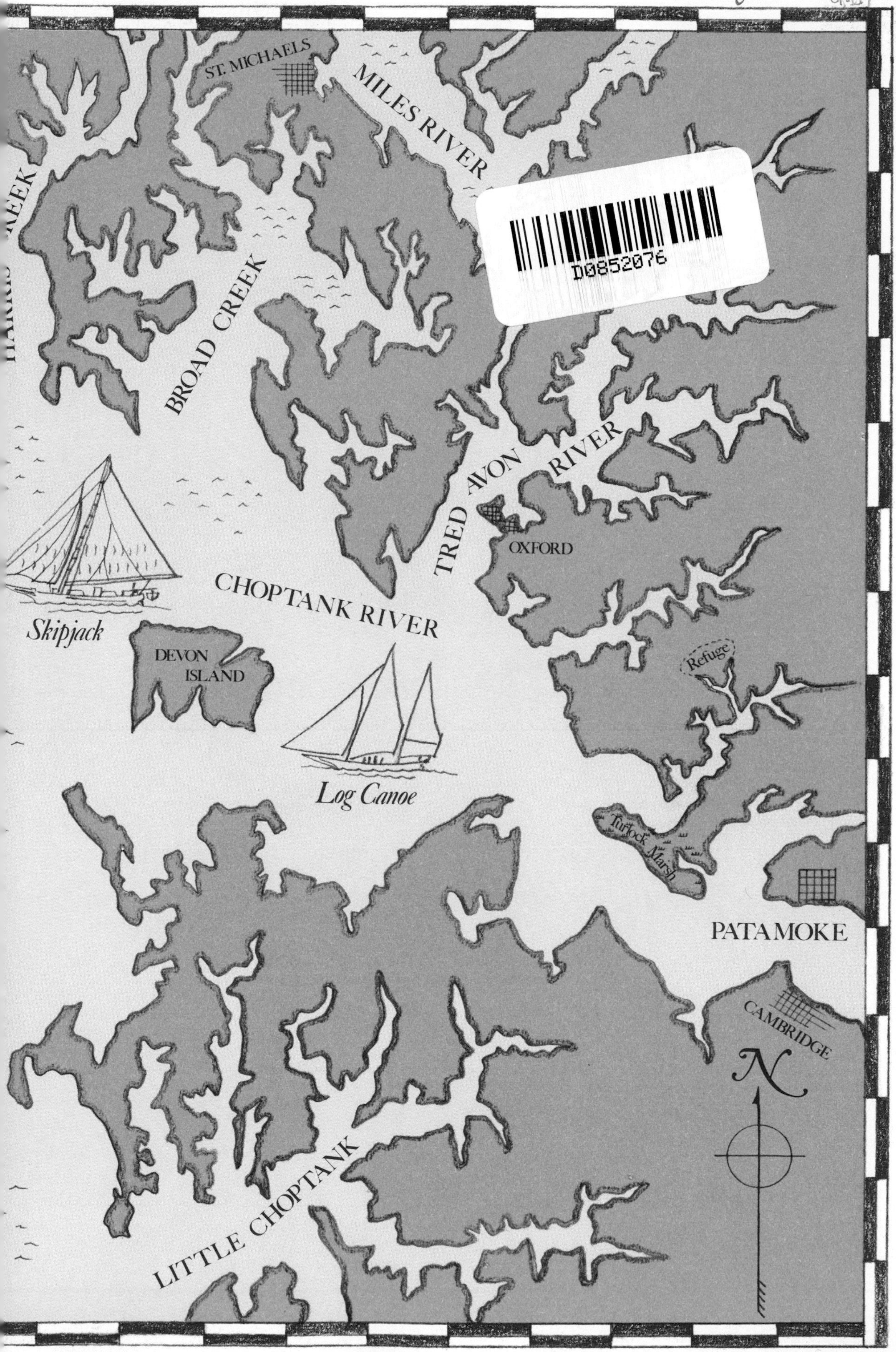

ST. MICHAELS

MILES RIVER

CREEK

BROAD CREEK

TRED AVON RIVER

OXFORD

CHOPTANK RIVER

Skipjack

DEVON ISLAND

Refuge

Log Canoe

Turlock Marsh

PATAMOKE

CAMBRIDGE

N

LITTLE CHOPTANK

THE
WATERMEN

THE
WATERMEN

Selections from *Chesapeake* *by*

JAMES A. MICHENER

With drawings made for this book by

JOHN MOLL

RANDOM HOUSE   NEW YORK

Library of Congress Cataloging in Publication Data

Michener, James Albert, 1907–
The watermen.

A narrative consisting of excerpts from the author's Chesapeake.
1.   Eastern Shore, Md.—History—Fiction.
I.   Moll, John.   II.   Title.
PZ3.M583Wat   [PS3525.I19]   813'.5'4   79–14119
ISBN 0–394–50660–X

First Edition

Contents

Foreword

FOR MANY YEARS I HAVE HOPED THAT SOME DAY ONE OF MY books would appear in an illustrated edition, principally because I admire the lovely way in which a page of well-printed text can combine with a woodcut, an engraving, an etching, a lithograph or a drawing. When well done, such a union seems to have been preordained.

I remember how much, as a boy, I enjoyed Arthur Rackham's illustrations and the visual impact of books by Lynd Ward and Rockwell Kent. I always loved the earlier works of Dickens and Thackeray, but I was quite content to see the sentimental 'illustrated novel' of the 1920's fall into disuse.

I had pretty well given up the thought that any book of mine could be so presented, but as I worked on the Eastern Shore on my novel *Chesapeake*, I became aware of an artist living not far from me whose work not only captured the flavor of my subject but had earned the enthusiasm of those who love the Chesapeake.

He is John Moll, who occupies a waterfront home in the colorful town of Oxford, where he has been producing a series of handsome drawings depicting the boats, the landscape and the wildlife of his area. He is a quiet man, and unfortunately for me, I had never had occasion to meet him. We were occupied with different matters.

But when I was about two-thirds of the way through my novel, and into the part I enjoyed most—the watermen—it suddenly occurred to me that my long-ago hope would be realized if John Moll could apply his gifted pencil to the story I was telling. It was impractical, of course, for I was engaged in a very long book in which there would be no space whatever for illustrations, even of the highest quality. So I said nothing to my editors or to Moll.

When the book was done and accepted by those who know the Chesapeake well, especially those watermen with whom I had worked aboard their boats, the nagging thought returned, so one wintry day I got into my car, drove down to Oxford, knocked on Moll's door, introduced myself and said, 'Would you be interested in illustrating one of my stories from *Chesapeake*?' He'd heard of the book but hadn't yet read it. When he did, he called me and said he would be happy to do it.

But there is another reason why I wanted to do this particular book, compiled from the watermen passages of *Chesapeake*. During the two years I worked on the bay I became more and more aware of what a dangerous life these men live: twice I was caught in storms of unbelievable suddenness and fury. Also during that time the local newspapers reported that twenty-one watermen lost their lives in our capricious bay. A skipjack, which is a large boat, turned end over end and six men went down. A crabber of the very best design and construction capsized and five watermen were drowned. A sudden gale swept up the bay and three different boats sank. A man on shore saw his boat starting to drift away, jumped in to save it, and was seen no more.

The Chesapeake is a wonderful vacation spot on a quiet summer's day, but it can be an unforgiving tyrant that same night when the winds rise. The men who work it are quiet heroes, echoes of that day long distant when most Americans made their living close to nature. They live with blistering heat and raw cold, with deer that graze in the meadow next to the house and geese that come down from Canada.

I wanted to do this book to let them know how much I respect them. John Moll has shown them at their work. He and I know every man who posed, unknowingly, for these pictures.

JAMES A. MICHENER
Broad Creek, 1979

The Geese

IN THE REMOTE WASTES OF NORTHERN CANADA, WHERE MAN WAS rarely seen except when lost and about to perish, a family of great geese, in the late summer of 1822, made their home on a forlorn stretch of Arctic moorland. Mother, father, six fledglings: because of a freak of nature they had come to a moment of terrifying danger.

The two adult birds, splendid heavy creatures weighing close to fourteen pounds and with wings normally capable of carrying them five thousand miles in flight, could not get off the ground. At a time when they had to feed and protect their offspring, they were powerless to fly. This was no accident, nor the result of any unfortunate experience with wolves; like all their breed they lost their heavy wing feathers every summer and remained earthbound for about six weeks, during which they could only hide from their enemies and walk ineffectively over the moorland, waiting for their feathers to return. It was for this reason that they had laid their eggs in such a remote spot, for during their moulting period they were almost defenseless.

Onk-or, the father in this family, strutted about the bushes seeking seeds, while his mate stayed near the nest to tend the fledglings, whose appetites were insatiable. Occasionally when Onk-or brought food to the younglings, his mate would run long distances as if pleased to escape the drudgery of her brood, but on this day when she reached the top of a grassy mound she ran faster, flapped the wings she had not used for six weeks and flew back toward her nest, uttering loud cries as she did so.

Onk-or looked up, saw the flight and sensed that within a day or two he would be soaring too; always her feathers grew back faster than his. As she flew past he spoke to her.

Maintaining a medium altitude, she headed north to where an arm of the sea intruded, and there she landed on water, splashing it ahead of her when her feet slammed down to act as brakes. Other geese landed to eat the seeds floating on the waves, and after weeks of loneliness she enjoyed their companionship, but before long she rose on the water, flapped her long wings slowly, gathered speed amidst great splashing, then soared into the air, heading back to her nest. From long habit, she landed short of where her fledglings lay, moved about unconcernedly to deceive any foxes that might be watching, then collected bits of food, which she carried to her children. As soon as she appeared, Onk-or walked away, still unable to fly, to gather more food.

He and his mate were handsome birds, large and sleek. Both they and their children had long necks feathered in jet-black, with a broad snow-white bib under the chin and reaching to the ears. When their wings were folded, as they were most of the time, the heavy body was compact and beautifully proportioned, and they walked with dignity, not waddling from side to side like ducks. Their heads were finely proportioned, with bills pointed but not grotesquely long, and the lines of their bodies, where feathers of differing shades of gray joined, were pleasing. Indeed, their subdued coloring was so appropriate to the Arctic moorland that an observer, had there been one, could have come close to their nest without noticing them.

On this day there was an observer, an Arctic fox who had not eaten for some time and was beginning to feel the urge of hunger. When from a distance he spotted the rough nest on the ground, with the six fledglings tumbling about and obviously not prepared to fly, he took no precipitate action, for he had learned respect for the sharp beaks and powerful wings of full-grown geese like Onk-or.

Instead he retreated and ran in large circles far from the nest, until he roused another fox to make the hunt with him. Together they returned quietly across the tundra, moving from the security of one tussock to the next, scouting the terrain ahead and developing the strategy they would use to pick off these young geese.

During the brightest part of the day they lay in wait, for long ago they had learned that it was easier to attack at night, when they would be less conspicuous against the Arctic grass. Of course, during the nesting season of the geese there was no real night; the sun stayed in the heavens permanently, scudding low in the north but never disappearing. Instead of blackness, which would last interminably during the winter, there came only a diffused grayness in the middle hours, a ghostly penumbra, with geese, young and old, half asleep. That was the time to attack.

So as the sun drifted lower in the west, on a long, sliding trajectory that would never dip below the horizon, and as the bright glare of summer faded to an exquisite gray matching the feathers of the geese, the two foxes moved slowly toward the nest where the six fledglings hid beneath the capacious wings of their mother. Onk-or, the foxes noted, lay some distance away with his head under his left wing.

It was the plan of the foxes that the stronger of the pair would attack Onk-or from such a direction that the big male goose would be lured even farther from the nest, and as the fight progressed, the other fox would dart in, engage the female briefly, and while she was awkwardly trying to defend herself, grab one of the young geese and speed away. In the confusion the first fox might very well be able to grab a second fledgling for himself. If not, they would share the one they did get.

When the foxes had attained a strategic position, the first made a lunge at Onk-or, attacking from the side on which he had tucked his head, on the logical supposition that if the great goose were not instantly alert, the fox might be lucky and grab him by the throat, ending that part of the fight then and there. But as soon as the fox accelerated his pace, knocking aside grasses, Onk-or was awake and

aware of what was happening. He did not try evasive action or do anything unusual to protect his neck; instead he pivoted on his left leg, swung his moulted wing in a small circle and with its bony edge knocked his adversary flat.

Onk-or knew that the fox would try to lure him away from the nest, so instead of following up on his first blow, he retreated toward the low pile of sticks and grass that constituted his nest, making sharp clicking sounds to alert his family. His mate, aware that the family was being attacked, drew the fledglings under her wings and studied the ominous grayness.

She did not have long to wait. As the first fox lunged at Onk-or again, the second swept in to attack the nest itself. She had only one flashing moment to ascertain from which direction the attack was coming, but she judged accurately, rose, spread her wings and pivoted to meet the fox. As he leaped at her, she struck him across the face with her powerful beak, stunning him momentarily.

He soon recovered to make a second attack. This time she was prepared, and a harsh swipe of her wing edge sent him sprawling, but this terrified her, for instinct warned her that he may cunningly have seemed to fall so as to distract her. If she struck at him now, he would slyly dart behind her and grab one of the fledglings. So as the fox fell, she wheeled on her right foot, placing herself and her extended wings between him and the nest. As for the rear, she had to depend upon Onk-or to protect that from the other fox.

This he was doing. In the half-light he fought the clever fox, fending him off with vicious stabs of his beak, knocking him down with his powerful wing thrusts and filling the Arctic air with short cries of rage and challenge. The fox, who had never been confident that he could subdue a grown male goose, began to lose any hope that he could even hold his own against this infuriated bird. Furthermore, he saw that his partner had accomplished nothing at the nest and was, indeed, absorbing an equal thrashing.

Hoping in vain that the two geese would make some fatal mistake, the two foxes battled on for a while, recognized the futility of their attack and withdrew, making short, chattering noises to one another as they did.

When daylight came the two parent geese knew how necessary it was that their six children proceed with the business of flying. So on this day Onk-or did not leave the nest to forage for his family; he stayed by the odd collection of twigs and grasses and nudged his children out onto the moorland, watching them as they clumsily tried their wings.

They were an ungainly lot, stumbling and falling and vainly beating their long wings, but gradually attaining the mastery which would enable them to fly south to the waters of Maryland. Two of the young birds actually hoisted themselves into the air, staying aloft for short distances, then landing with maximum awkwardness and joy.

A third, watching the success of her siblings, flapped her wings clumsily, ran across the rocky ground and with great effort got herself into the air, but as soon as she did so, Onk-or felt a rush of terror, for he saw something she did not.

Too late! The gosling, unable to maintain flight, fluttered heavily to the ground, landing precisely where the two foxes had been waiting for such a misadventure. But as they started for the fallen bird, Onk-or, with supreme effort, flapped his wings not yet ready for flight, rose in the air and endeavored to smash down at the foxes. His wings were not equal to the task, and he, too, fell, but before the dust was gone from his eyes he was on his feet, charging at the two foxes. Insolently, the first fox grabbed the gosling, killing it with one savage snap of the jaws, and sped away. The second fox ran in circles, tantalizing Onk-or, then disappeared to join his partner in their feast.

What did this family of seven think as they reassembled? Onk-or and his mate were unusual in the animal kingdom in that they mated for life. They were as tightly married as any human couple in Patamoke; each cared desperately what happened to the other, and Onk-or would unhesitatingly sacrifice his life to protect that of his mate. Four times they had flown together down from the Arctic to the Eastern Shore, and four times back. Together they had located safe resting spots up and down eastern Canada and in all the seaboard states of America. Aloft, they communicated instinctively, each knowing what the other intended, and on the ground, either when nesting in the Arctic or feeding along the Choptank, each always felt responsible for the safety of the other.

In this habit of permanent marriage they were like few other birds, certainly not like the lesser ducks who mated at will, staying close to each other only so long as their ducklings needed protection. It was a curiosity peculiar to the great geese. Beavers also married for life—perhaps because they had to live together during their winters in lodges frozen over—but few other animals. Onk-or was married to his mate, eternally.

His first response, therefore, as the foxes disappeared with one of his daughters, was an intuitive checking to assure himself that his mate was safe. Satisfied on this crucial point, his attention shifted to his five remaining children. They must learn to fly—now—and not stumble into traps set by enemies.

His mate, who had remained on the ground during the loss of the fledgling, had not been able to ascertain what was happening with the foxes, for the incident had occurred behind a cluster of tussocks, and for one dreadful moment she had feared that it might be he the foxes had taken. She was relieved when she saw him stumbling back, for he was half her life, the gallant, fearless bird on whom she must depend.

But she also possessed a most powerful urge to protect her offspring; she would surrender her own life to achieve this, and now the first of them had been stolen. She did not grieve, as she would have done had Onk-or been killed, but she did feel a dreadful sense of loss, and like her mate, determined that the other five must quickly learn to fly. In the days to come she would be a ruthless teacher.

As for the goslings, each knew that a fox had stolen the missing child. Each knew that tragedy, from which their parents tried to protect them, had struck, and the nascent urges which had caused them to attempt flight were intensified. They had never made the long pilgrimage to the feeding grounds of Maryland, but intuitively knew that such grounds must be somewhere and they should ready themselves for the incredible migration. They were determined to master their wings; they were determined to protect themselves from foxes.

Of course, these birds were too young to have selected partners, nor had they associated with other geese. But even at this early stage they were aware of the difference between the sexes, so that the three young males were looking for something quite different from what the two remaining females were awaiting, and as other families of geese flew overhead, each fledgling could differentiate the children in that tentative flock. They knew. At seven weeks it was incredible what these young geese knew, and if by some ill chance both their parents should be killed, leaving them orphaned in the Arctic, they would know how to fly to Maryland and find the Choptank cove that had been designated as their home. All they needed for maturity was the strengthening of their wings and the selection of a mate from the other fledglings born that year. They were a doughty breed, one of the great birds of the world, and they behaved so.

In mid-September, as in each year of their lives, Onk-or and his mate felt irresistible urgings. They watched the sky and were particularly responsive to the shortening of the day. They noticed with satisfaction that their five children were large and powerful birds, with notable wing spans and sustaining accumulations of fat; they were ready for any flight. They also noticed the browning of the grasses and the ripening of certain seeds, signs unmistakable that departure was imminent.

At all the nests in the Arctic this restlessness developed and birds bickered with one another. Males would suddenly rise in the sky and fly long distances for no apparent reason, returning later to land in clouds of dust. No meetings were held; there was no visible assembling of families. But one day, for mysterious reasons which could not be explained, huge flocks of birds rose into the sky, milled about and then formed into companies heading south.

This southward migration was one of the marvels of nature: hundreds, thousands, millions of these huge geese forming into perfect V-shaped squadrons flying at different altitudes and at different times of day, but all heading out of Canada down one of the four principal flyways leading to varied corners of America. Some flew at 29,000 feet above the ground, others as low as 3,000, but all sought escape from the freezing moorlands of the Arctic, heading for clement feeding grounds like those in Maryland. For long spells they would fly in silence, but most often they maintained noisy communication, arguing, protesting, exulting; at night especially they uttered cries which echoed forever in the memories of men who heard them drifting down through the frosty air of autumn: *'Onk-or, onk-or!'*

The wedge in which Onk-or and his family started south this year consisted of eighty-nine birds, but it did not stay together permanently as a cohesive unit. Sometimes other groups would meld with it, until the flying formation contained several hundred birds; at other times segments would break away to fly with some other unit. But in general the wedge held together.

The geese flew at a speed of about forty-five miles an hour, which meant that if they stayed aloft for an entire day, they could cover a thousand miles. But they required rest, and through the centuries during which they had followed the same route south and north they had learned of various ponds and lakes and riverbanks which afforded them secure places to rest and forage. There were lakes in upper Quebec, and small streams leading into the St. Lawrence. In Maine there were hundreds of options and suitable spots in western Massachusetts and throughout New York, and the older geese like Onk-or knew them all.

On some days, near noon when the autumn sun was high, the geese would descend abruptly and alight on a lake which their ancestors had been utilizing for thousands of years. The trees along the shore would have changed, and new generations of fish would occupy the waters, but the seeds would be the same kind, and the succulent grasses. Here the birds would rest for six or seven hours, and then as dusk approached, the leaders would utter signals and the flock would scud across the surface of the lake, wheel into the air and fly aloft. There they would form themselves automatically into a long V, with some old, sage bird like Onk-or in the lead, and through the night they would fly south.

Maine, New Hampshire, Massachusetts, Connecticut, New York, Pennsylvania! The states would lie sleeping below, only a few dim lamps betraying their existence, and overhead the geese would go, crying in the night, '*Onk-or, onk-or*,' and occasionally, at the edge of some village or on some farm a door would open and light would flood the area for a while, and parents would hold their children and peer into the dark sky, listening to the immortal passing of the geese. And once in a great while, on such a night, when the moon was full, the children would actually see the flying wedge pass between them and the moon, and hear the geese as they flew, and this matter they would speak of for the rest of their lives.

No goose, not even a powerful one like Onk-or, could fly at the head of the wedge for long periods. The buffeting of the wind as the point of the V broke a path through the air turbulence was too punishing. The best a practiced bird could do was about forty minutes, during which time he absorbed a considerable thrashing. After his allotted time in the lead position, the exhausted goose would drop to the back of one of the arms of the wedge, where the weaker birds had been assembled, and there, with the air well broken ahead of him, he would coast along in the wake of the others, recovering his strength until it came his time again to assume the lead. Male and female alike accepted this responsibility, and when the day's flight ended, they were content to rest. On especially favorable lakes with copious feed they might stay for a week.

During the first days of October the geese were usually somewhere in New York or Pennsylvania, and happy to be there. The sun was warm and the lakes congenial, but as the northwest winds began to blow, bringing frost at night, the older birds grew restive. They did not relish a sudden freeze, which would present problems, and they vaguely knew that the waning of the sun required them to be farther south in some region of security.

But they waited until the day came when the air was firmly frosted, and then they rose to form their final V. No matter where the lake had been upon which they were resting, the geese in the eastern flyway vectored in to the Susquehanna River, and when they saw its broad and twisting silhouette, they felt safe. This was their immemorial guide, and they followed it with assurance, breaking at last onto the Chesapeake, the most considerable body of water they would see during their migration. It shimmered in the autumn sun and spoke of home. Its thousand estuaries and coves promised them food and refuge for the long winter, and they joyed to see it.

As soon as the Chesapeake was reached, congregations of geese began to break off, satisfied that they had arrived at their appointed locations. Four thousand would land at Havre de Grace, twenty thousand at the Sassafras. The Chester River would lure more than a hundred thousand and the Miles the same. Enormous concentrations would elect Tred Avon, but the most conspicuous aggregation would wait for the Choptank, more than a quarter of a million birds, and they would fill every field and estuary.

For more than five thousand years Onk-or's lineal antecedents had favored a marsh on the north bank of the Choptank. It was spacious, well-grassed with many plants producing seeds, and multiple channels providing safe hiding places. It was convenient both to fields, so that the geese could forage for seeds, and to the river, so that they could land and take off easily. It was an ideal wintering home in every respect but one: it was owned by the Turlocks, the most inveterate hunters of Maryland, each member of the family born with an insatiable appetite for goose.

'I can eat it roasted, or chopped with onions and peppers, or sliced thin with mushrooms,' Lafe Turlock was telling the men at the store. 'You can keep the other months of the year, just give me November with a fat goose comin' onto the stove three times a week.'

Lafe had acquired from his father and his father before him the secrets of hunting geese. 'Canniest birds in the world. They have a sixth sense, a seventh and an eighth. I've seen one smart old gander haunts my place lead his flock right into my blind, spot my gun, stop dead in the air, turn his whole congregation around on a six-pence, without me gettin' a shot.' He kicked the stove and volunteered his summary of the situation: 'A roast goose tastes so good because it's so danged hard to shoot.'

'Why's that?' a younger hunter asked.

Lafe turned to look at the questioner, studied him contemptuously as an interloper, then explained, 'I'll tell you what, sonny, I know your farm down the river. Fine farm for huntin' geese. Maybe a hundred thousand fly past in the course of a week, maybe two hundred thousand. But that ain't doin' you no good, because unless you can tease just one of those geese to drop down within gunshot of where you stand, you ain't never gonna kill a goose. They fly over there'—he flailed his long arms—'or over here, or down there, a hundred thousand geese in sight . . .' He startled the young man by leaping from his chair and banging his fist against the wall. 'But never one goddamned goose where you want him. It's frustratin'.'

He sat down, cleared his throat and spoke like a lawyer presenting a difficult case. 'So what you got to do, sonny, is pick yourself a likely spot where they might land, and build yourself a blind—'

'I done that.'

Lafe ignored the interruption. 'And hide it in branches that look live, and all round it put wooden decoys whittled into at least eight different positions to look real, and then learn to yell goose cries that would fool the smartest goose ever lived. And if you don't do all these things, sonny, you ain't never gonna taste goose, because they gonna fly past you, night and day.'

The attractive thing about Lafe was his unquenchable enthusiasm. Each October, like now, he was convinced that this year he would outsmart the geese, and he was not afraid to make his predictions public at the store. 'This year, gentlemen, you all eat goose. I'm gonna shoot so many, your fingers'll grow warts pluckin' 'em.'

'That's what you said last year,' an uncharitable waterman grunted.

'But this year I got me a plan.' And with a finger dipped in molasses he started to outline his strategy. 'You know my blind out in the river.'

'I stood there often enough, gettin' nothin',' one of the men said.

'And you know this blind at that pond in the western end of the marsh.'

'I waited there for days and all I got was a wet ass,' the same man said.

'And that's what you'll get in that blind this year, too. Because I'm settin' them two up just like always, decoys and all. I want that smart old leader to see them and lead his ladies away.'

'To where?' the skeptic asked.

Lafe grinned and a deep satisfaction wreathed his face. 'Now for my plan. Over here, at the edge of this cornfield where everythin' looks so innicent, I plant me a third blind with the best decoys me or my pappy ever carved.' And with a dripping finger he allowed the molasses to form his new blind.

'I don't think it'll work,' the cynic said.

'I'm gonna get me so many geese . . .'

'Like last year. How many you get last year, speak honest.'

'I got me nine geese . . .' In six months he had shot nine geese, but this year, with his new tactics, he was sure to get scores.

So when Onk-or brought his wedge of eighty-nine back to the Choptank marshes, dangerous innovations awaited. Of course, on his first pass over Turlock land he spotted the traditional blind in the river and the ill-concealed one at the pond; generations of his family had been avoiding those inept seductions. He also saw the same old decoys piled on the bank, the boats waiting to take the hunters into the river and the dogs waiting near the boats. It was familiar and it was home.

Giving a signal, he dropped in a tight, crisp circle, keeping his left wing almost stationary, then landed with a fine splashing on an opening in the center of the marsh. He showed his five children how to dispose themselves, then pushed his way through the marsh grass to see for himself what feed there might be in the fields. His mate came along, and within a few minutes they had satisfied themselves that this was going to be a good winter. On their way back to the marsh they studied the cabin. No changes there; same wash behind the kitchen.

As the geese settled in to enjoy the marshes, the young birds heard for the first time the reverberation of gunfire, and Onk-or

had to spend much time alerting them to the special dangers that accompanied these rich feeding grounds. He and the other ganders taught the newcomers how to spot the flash of metal, or hear the cracking of a twig under a gunner's boot. And no group must ever feed without posting at least three sentinels, whose job it was to keep their necks erect so that their ears and eyes could scout all approaches.

Eternal vigilance was the key to survival, and no birds ever became more skilled in protecting themselves. Smaller birds, like doves, which presented difficult targets for a hunter, could often trust to luck that an undetected human would miss when he fired at them, but the great goose presented such an attractive target either head-on or broadside that a gunner had the advantage, if he were allowed to creep within range. The trick for the geese was to move out of range whenever men approached, and Onk-or drilled his flock assiduously in this tactic, for any goose who frequented the Turlock marshes was threatened by some of the most determined hunters on the Eastern Shore.

By mid-December it was clear that the geese had outsmarted Lafe Turlock once again; none had landed at the blind in the river and only a few stragglers had landed at the pond. By the end of the first week Onk-or had spotted the cornfield trick, and Lafe had been able to shoot only three geese.

'Them damn honkers must of got eyeglasses in Canada,' he told the men at the store.

'You was gonna feed us all this winter,' one of the men reminded him.

'I will, too. What I got to do is make a few changes in my plan.'

He assembled his five sons, plus four other crack shots, and told them, 'We are gonna get ourselves so many geese, you'll have grease on your faces all winter. We do it this way.'

An hour before dawn he rowed his youngest son out to the river blind, before which they strung a dozen decoys haphazardly. He told his boy, 'I want for the geese to see you. Make 'em move on.'

Another son he placed at the pond, with the same careless arrangement and the same instructions. 'Of course, son, if you get a good shot at a goose, take it. But we ain't relyin' on you.'

At the cornfield he posted yet a third son, expecting him to be seen. The six other men he took on a long walk through loblolly, ending at a cove where he said the canny geese would have to land. 'The trick is to think like a goose. They'll leave the cornfield, fly in a half-circle, see the decoys beyond the pine trees and come down here.'

When they came down, they were going to land in the middle of a fusillade from the four fastest guns, followed immediately by a second round from the three slower guns, during which time the first four would load again to pick off the cripples, by which time the slow guns could reload to do any cleaning up.

'This is guaranteed to get honkers,' Lafe promised, 'if'n that damned big bird don't catch on.'

The geese were slow this morning in going to their feeding stations. There was fractiousness among the younger birds, but the elders did not protest, for mating time was approaching and there were many second-year geese who had not yet selected their partners, so that confusion was inescapable. But toward six-thirty Onk-or and another old gander began making the moves that would get the flock started. Restlessness ceased and eighty-odd birds began moving into positions from which they could take to the air.

Onk-or led the flight, and within moments the flock had formed into two loose Vs which wheeled and dipped in unison. They headed for the river south of the marsh, and Onk-or saw that some hunter was still trying vainly to lure geese into the old blind located there. The big birds landed well upstream, fed for a while on grasses, then took off for better forage. They flew to the pond, where there was futile gunfire, and then toward the cornfield, where Onk-or quickly spotted the lone gunner stationed there. He swung away from the corn, flew left, and saw some geese feeding in a stream lined by pine trees. Since the geese already down proved that the area was safe, he would land his flock there.

The geese came in low, wings extended, feet ready for braking, but just as Onk-or prepared to land, he detected movement among the pine trees lining the shore, and with a brilliant twist to the

north he swung out of range, uttering loud cries of warning as he did so. He escaped, and those immediately behind made their turns, too, but many of the trailing geese did not react in time; they flew directly into the waiting guns and furious blasts of fire knocked them down.

Seven geese were killed, including two of Onk-or's children. It was a disaster, and he had been responsible. It must not happen again.

At the store Lafe basked in his victory. 'To catch a honker you got to think like a honker,' he told his listeners, but his glory was short-lived, because for the rest of the season he got no geese from his own marshes, and only two when he led an expedition farther upstream.

'I never seen honkers so cagey,' he snarled. 'I'm goin' to hire me them trolls from Amos Todkill.' So in January 1823 he sailed up to Patamoke to dicker with Todkill, who specialized in combing the marshes for wounded young geese, which he domesticated, using them as living lures to bring wild geese directly into the muzzles of waiting guns.

Todkill said he'd allow Turlock to rent fifteen of his tame geese, three days for a dollar and a half. 'Pretty steep,' Lafe complained.

'But you know they're foolproof. "Never-fails," we call 'em.'

Turlock tied their legs, tossed them into his boat and sailed back to the marsh. 'I want me fifteen or sixteen reliable guns,' he announced at the store. 'I laid out real money for them damned trolls, and I expect some honkers in return.'

He enlisted a veritable battery, whose members he stationed at strategic spots so that the crossfire from the muzzle-loaders would be impenetrable. He then spread four dozen of his most lifelike wooden decoys, after which he released Todkill's fifteen live ones. 'As pretty a sight as a honker ever seen, and as deadly,' he said approvingly when all was in position.

Then he and the sixteen other hunters waited. Nothing happened. Occasional geese from the marshes flew past, ignoring the trolls, who cackled to lure them down. Once or twice substantial flocks, headed by the old gander, came tantalizingly close, then veered away as if in obedience to a signal, and the three days passed without one good shot at a honker.

Onk-or from the first had spotted the bizarre assembly of wooden decoys and live trolls, and it was not long before he discerned the guns hiding among the rushes. He not only kept his own geese from the lethal area; he also alerted others, so that Lafe and his artillery could not possibly get themselves the geese he had promised.

At the store one of the hunters said, 'Them trolls fooled me, and they fooled Lafe, but they sure as hell didn't fool that old gander.'

'What they did,' Lafe said, 'was waste my dollar-fifty. It was only through the help of prayer that I kept from stranglin' them birds before I gave 'em back to Todkill."

The men laughed. The idea of Lafe Turlock's hurting a goose, except to shoot it, was preposterous. He loved the big birds, fed them cracked corn when snow covered the ground, rescued cripples at the end of the season and turned them over to Todkill. Once, after a big revival meeting, he said, 'The life of man is divided into two seasons: "Geese is here. Geese ain't here."' So when the men joshed him over his costly failure, they were surprised that he did not fight back.

He remained silent for a good reason: he was ready to shift into phase three of his grand design. Assembling his sons in early March, he told them, 'Turlocks eat geese because we're smarter'n geese. And a danged sight smarter'n them dummies at the store, because I know somethin' that would rile 'em, if'n they had brains to understand.'

His sons waited. He looked out the door at the March sky and confided, 'I been trampin' through the woods, and I think I found me the spot where they does their courtin'.' He was referring to those few geese who had either been wounded by ineffective gun-fire or seduced by the clemency of the Choptank; they would not be flying north with the others, but would remain behind, raising their Maryland-born families in marshes to the south. And when they mated, they would be vulnerable, for as Lafe explained to his sons, 'Geese is just like men. When their minds get fixed on ass, caution goes out the window, and come next week we're gonna knock down enough careless geese to feed us through July.'

It was in the deepest nature of a Turlock to be sanguine where hunting and fishing were concerned: the oysters were down there but they could be tonged; the crabs might be hiding but they could be caught. 'How we gonna do it, Pop?'

'Strategy,' Lafe said.

Onk-or, too, was thinking strategy. He must get his flock through the frenzy of this season without loss, and to accomplish this he must keep them away from the mating grounds, for he had learned that when young geese gawked at their contemporaries in the mating dance, they grew inattentive, and their elders were no better, for they, too, stood about cackling and enjoying the proceedings, unmindful of lurking guns.

So for both Lafe and Onk-or the last days of winter became critical, for the man had to find the mating ground, and the goose had to keep his family away from it. Nine days went by without a loss to the Turlock guns.

'No fear,' Lafe assured his boys. 'Honkers has got to mate, and when they do, we come into our own.'

He had anticipated, almost better than the young geese, where those who did not fly north would conduct their courtships, and there, along a grassy field deep in the woods, he placed himself and his sons, each with three muskets. The young geese, responding to their own inner urgings, were drawn to this spot, and there they began their dances.

Two males would focus upon one female, who would stand aside, shyly preening herself, as if she held a mirror. She would keep her eyes on the ground, pretending to ignore events which would determine how she would live for the remainder of her life.

The males meanwhile grew more and more active, snapping at each other and hissing, advancing and retreating and putting on a great show of fury. Finally one would actually attack the other, flailing with wings extended six or seven feet, and crashing heavy blows upon the head and shoulders of the other. Now the fight became real, with each heavy bird attempting to grab the other's head in its powerful beak.

According to some intricate scoring system, it would become apparent to both contestants, to the rest of the flock and especially to the waiting female that one of the fighting birds had triumphed. The other would retreat, and then would come the most moving part of the dance.

The victorious male would approach the waiting female with mincing steps, swaying from side to side, and as he drew near he would extend his neck to the fullest and gently wave it back and forth, close to the chosen one, and she would extend hers, and they would intertwine, rarely touching, and they would stand thus, weaving and twisting their necks in one of the most delicate and graceful manifestations in nature.

As the dance approached its climax, the young geese of Onk-or's group started instinctively toward the mating ground, and although Onk-or and his mate moved frantically to intercept them, they bumbled their way into the open area.

'Now!' Turlock signaled, and the guns blazed. Before the startled geese could take to the air, the six Turlocks dropped their guns, grabbed others and blazed away, dropped them and reached for their back-ups. Geese fell in startling numbers, and by the time Onk-or could get his flock into the air, enough lay dead to stock the icehouse.

When they reassembled in the marsh Onk-or discovered that one of his sons was dead, and he was about to lament when he found to his terror that his wife was missing, too. He had seen geese falter and fall into the grass offshore, and he knew intuitively that the men would now be combing that margin to find the cripples.

Without hesitation he left his flock and sped back to the mating ground. His arrival disconcerted the men who, as he had expected, were searching for wounded birds. Flying directly over their heads, he landed in the area at which he had seen the geese falling, and there he found his mate, sorely crippled in the left wing. It was impossible for her to fly, and within minutes the dogs and men would find her.

Urging her with heavy pushes of his bill, he shoved her through ill-defined waterways, heading her always toward the safety of the deeper marshes. When she faltered, he pecked at her feathers, never allowing her to stop.

They had progressed about two hundred yards when a mongrel yellow dog with an especially good nose came upon their scent and realized that he had a cripple somewhere in the bushes ahead. Silently he made his way ever closer to the wounded goose, until, with a final leap, he was upon her.

What he did not anticipate was that she was accompanied by a full-grown gander determined to protect her. Suddenly, from the water near the cripple, Onk-or rose up, whipped his heavy beak about and slashed at the dog. The startled animal withdrew in shock, then perceived the situation and lunged at the gander.

A deadly, splashing fight ensued, with the dog having every advantage. But Onk-or marshaled all his powers; he was fighting not only to protect himself but also to save his crippled mate, and deep in the tangled marsh he attacked the dog with a confusing flash of wing and thrust of beak. The dog retreated.

'There's a cripple in there!' Turlock shouted to his sons. 'Tiger's got hisse'f a cripple.'

But the dog appeared with nothing except a bleeding cut on the head. 'Hey! Tiger's been hit by a honker. Get in there and find that cripple.'

Three boys and their dogs splashed into the marsh, but by this time Onk-or had guided his damaged mate to safety. They hid among the rushes as the men splashed noisily, while the mongrels, not eager to encounter whatever had struck Tiger, made little attempt to find them.

A week later, when the crippled wing had mended, Onk-or herded his geese together and they started their mandatory flight to the Arctic: Pennsylvania, Connecticut, Maine, and then the frozen moorlands of Canada. One night as they flew over a small town in central New York they made a great honking, and citizens came out to follow their mysterious passage. Among them was a boy of eight. He stared at the shadowy forms and listened to their distant conversation. As a consequence of this one experience he would become attached to birds, would study all things about them, and in his adult life would paint them and write about them and take the first steps in providing sanctuaries for them, and all because on one moonlit night he heard the geese pass overhead.

The Storm

THE WORST STORMS TO HIT THE CHESAPEAKE ARE THE HURRI-
canes which generate in the southeast, over the Atlantic
Ocean. There they twist and turn, building power and lifting from the waves enormous quantities of water that they carry
north in turbulent clouds.

They first hit Cape Charles, at the southern end of the Eastern
Shore, then explode ferociously over the waters of the bay, driving
crabbers and oystermen to shore. Their winds, often reaching a
fierce ninety miles an hour, whip the shallow waters of the Chesapeake into waves so violent that any small boat runs a good risk of
being capsized.

In late August of 1886 such a hurricane collected its force just
south of Norfolk, but instead of devastating the bay, it leapfrogged
far to the north, depositing in the Susquehanna Valley an incredible
fall of rain. In less than a day, nineteen inches fell on certain parts
of Pennsylvania, and all things were flooded, even into New York
State. Harrisburg felt the lash as its waterfront homes were submerged; Sunbury was inundated; poor Wilkes-Barre watched the
dark waters engulf its jetties; and even Towanda, far to the north,
was swamped by raging floods from streams that a day earlier had
been mere trickles.

From a thousand such rivulets the great flood accumulated, and as it crested on its way south to the Chesapeake, it buried small towns and endangered large cities. On it came, a devastating onslaught of angry water, twisting and probing into every depression. Past Harrisburg it swept, and Columbia, and over small villages near the border of Pennsylvania. Finally, in northern Maryland, it exploded with destructive fury into the body of the Chesapeake, raising the headwaters of that considerable bay four and five feet.

For three days the storm continued, producing strange and arbitrary results. Norfolk was by-passed completely: merely a heavy rain. Crisfield had no problems: a slow rain of no significance. Devon Island and Patamoke were barely touched: their biggest problem was that they had no sun during three days. But the great bay itself was nearly destroyed: it came close to being drowned by the floods cascading down from the north. It lay strangling in its own water.

To understand what was happening, one must visualize the bay as carefully structured in three distinct dimensions. From north to south the waters of the bay were meticulously graduated according to their salt content, and any alteration of this salinity was fraught with peril. At Havre de Grace, where the Susquehanna debouched into the bay, there should have been in autumn three parts of salt per thousand; there was none. On the oyster beds near Devon Island there ought to have been fifteen parts per thousand to keep the shellfish healthy; there were two. And at the crabbing beds farther south the crustaceans were accustomed to nineteen parts; they had to contend with less than six. All living things in the bay were imperiled, for the great flood had altered the bases of their existence. The protection provided by salt water was being denied them, and if relief did not come quickly, millions upon millions of bay creatures were going to die.

Prompt restoration of the traditional north-south relationship was essential, but the bay was also divided into a bottom and a top. The lowest area contained deep, cold, very salt water, often deficient in oxygen, moving in from the Atlantic Ocean, bringing many life-sustaining components. Deep down, it tended to move in a northerly direction, and its presence was essential for the health of the bay. On top rested the less salt, less heavy, warmer water replenished by the sun and containing a good oxygen content. It tended to move in a southward direction, sliding along on the top of the cold water. It carried with it many of the lesser forms of marine life on which the crabs and fish lived, and it deposited the nutrients which the oysters lower down required.

But these two vast layers of water should not be considered unrelated, like sheets of mutually exclusive steel moving in opposite directions, each independent of the other. Convection currents, generated by the sun, could at any given point draw the cold layer up and force the warm layer down. A strong surface wind might encourage such an interchange; the passing churning propeller of a large ship could augment the normal pressures that from below and above were constantly working on the two layers, causing them to mix.

But in general the water down deep was colder and saltier and slower; the water near the surface was warmer and less salty and more filled with oxygen. There was another difference: the water on the surface moved freely, even capriciously, over the entire surface of the bay; but the deep water held close to the invisible channel cut some hundred thousand years ago by the prehistoric Susquehanna as it drained away the waters of the first ice age. At the bottom of the Chesapeake, running its entire length and reaching well out into the Atlantic, this primeval riverbed existed, sixty feet deeper than the shallow waters surrounding it, but as clearly defined as when first reamed out by tumbling boulders.

Any sharp dislocation of the upper and lower levels of the bay would have disastrous consequences, for over the millennia marine life had learned to accommodate to the conditions as they existed, and there were many creatures living in the upper layer of warm, light water who could not survive if the cold, heavy water of the bottom suddenly engulfed them.

There was a final division, this one between the western half of the bay and the eastern. The former was fed by five substantial rivers—Patuxent, Potomac, Rappahannock, York, James—some of which drained large inland areas reaching westward to the Blue

Ridge Mountains. The huge flow of fresh water contributed by these rivers made the western half of the bay much less saline than the eastern, more silty, more filled with accidental non-marine vegetation, and in general more active.

The so-called rivers of the Eastern Shore did not deserve that name. They were not rivers in the customary sense: they drained no large upland areas; they had no great length; they had no fall; they did not collect fresh water from large drainage areas; they were tidal for most of their reach; and they were notably salty for much of their distance and brackish the rest. They were really tidal inlets —*estuaries* was the proper name—probing arms of the bay, which curled inland, creating flats and marshes.

Since they deposited only a fraction of the water produced by the western rivers, the eastern half of the bay had to be saltier, more torpid, more given to marshes, and much more productive of those small saltwater plants that sustained marine life. Also, another natural phenomenon contributed to the saltiness of the eastern half; the whirling motion of the earth applied a constant force that pushed the heavier water to the east, so that if a scientist drew isohalines—lines connecting all points west to east that had identical percentages of salt water—they would tilt conspicuously from southwest up to northeast. This meant that a line drawn due west from Devon Island, with its fifteen parts of salt per thousand, would find water much less salty in the middle of the bay and notably less so on the western shore. In fact, to find water on the western shore with a salinity equal to Devon's, one would have to drop twenty-five miles south.

Watermen skilled in reading the variations of the Chesapeake kept in mind that there were really three distinct segments: the moderately deep riverine western part; the very deep central channel followed by the steamers, which represented the course of the prehistoric and now drowned Susquehanna; and the exciting estuaries of the eastern portion, where plankton and menhaden and crabs and oysters abounded.

An Episcopal clergyman in Patamoke, with time on his hands and a fine Princeton education behind him, carried this analysis to its logical conclusion:

> We have three dimensions. North-south, west-east, top-bottom. If we divide each of these into ten gradations, 0 through 9, we can construct a numbering system which will locate precisely where we are in this diverse body of water. The northernmost, westernmost, shallowest point at that spot would be 0–0–0. The southernmost, easternmost, deepest point at that spot would be 9–9–9. Thus we really have one thousand distinct Chesapeakes. Devon Island, which is a focus for us, would be less than halfway down the bay from north to south and would be classified as 4. It stands not quite at the extreme eastern edge, so gets an 8. The bar where the oysters grow is at the bottom, which gives a 9. Therefore, the position in which we are interested is 4–8–9.

What happened in 1886 at Chesapeake Bay Number 4–8–9? The magnitude of this storm broke all existing records not by trivial percentages but by huge multipliers. For example, the greatest previous discharge of fresh water at the mouth of the Susquehanna had been something like 400,000 cubic feet per second, and that represented a devastating flood. Now the disgorgement was more than three times as great, an unheard of 1,210,000. This produced a volume of non-salt water so prodigious that it shifted the isohalines seventy-two miles southward, which meant that the waters about Devon Island had become practically salt-free.

When the storm broke, there existed on a small subterranean shelf at the western edge of Devon Island—point 4–8–9 by the clergyman's calculation—a congregation of oysters which had fastened themselves securely to the solid bottom. Here some of the largest and tastiest oysters of the bay had produced their generations, while the minute spat drifted back and forth with the slow currents until they fastened to the bottom to develop the shells in which they would grow during the years of their existence.

Along this shelf, well known to watermen from Patamoke but

kept by them as a secret, oysters had thrived during all the generations watermen had tonged the bay; no matter how many bushels of large oysters were lifted from this location, others replaced them. This was the shelf that could be depended upon.

In its original stages the flood from the Susquehanna did not affect these oysters. True, the salinity of all the water dropped, but at the depth at which they lived the loss did not, in these first days, imperil them. But there was another aspect of the flood which did. The Susquehanna, as it swept down from New York, picked up an astonishing burden of fine silt; for example, a house along the river-bank in Harrisburg might be inundated for only seven hours, but when the owners returned they would find in their second-floor bedrooms six inches of silt. How could it possibly have got there? Well, each cubic centimeter of seeping brown water carried its burden of almost invisible dust lifted from the farms of New York and Pennsylvania, and it was this dust, suspended in water, that was left behind.

The silt that fell in the bedroom of a butcher in Harrisburg could, when it dried, be swept away, but the silt which fell on a bed of oysters could not.

Down it came, silently, insidiously and very slowly. In four days more silt fell than in the previous sixty years. The entire Choptank as far east as Patamoke was chocolate-colored from the turbulent mud, but as soon as the waters began to calm themselves, their burden of silt was released and it fell persistently and inescapably onto the oysters.

At first it was no more than a film such as the propellers of the evening ferry might have deposited on any night. Such an amount caused no problem and might even bring with it plankton to feed the oysters. But this thin film was followed by a perceptible thickness, and then by more, until the oysters became agitated within their heavy shells. The spat, of course, were long since strangled. A whole oncoming generation of oysters had been suffocated.

Still the fine silt drifted down, an interminable rain of desolation. The bottom of the Choptank was covered with the gray-brown deposit; whole grains were so minute that the resulting mud seemed

more like cement, except that it did not harden; it merely smothered everything on which it fell, pressing down with fingers so delicate, its weight could not be felt until the moment it had occupied every space with a subtle force more terrible than a tower of stone.

The oysters could have withstood a similar intrusion of sand; then the particles would have been so coarse that water could continue to circulate and plankton be obtained. Submersion of even a month was tolerable, for in time the sand would wash away, leaving the shellfish no worse for their experience. But the flood-swept silt was another matter, and on the tenth day after the flood, when the brown waters bore their heaviest burden of mud, even the mature oysters on the Devon shelf began to die. No lively water was reaching them, no plankton. They were entombed in a dreadful cascade of silt and they could not propel themselves either to a new location or to a new level. Secured to their shelf, they had to rely on passing tides that would wash the silt away. But none came.

On the twelfth day the waters of the Chesapeake reached their maximum muddiness; silt from midland Pennsylvania was coming down now, in a final burst of destruction, and when it reached the relatively calm waters of the Choptank, it broke loose from its carrying waters and filtered slowly down to the bed of the river. This was the final blow. The oysters were already submerged under two inches of silt; now three more piled on, and one by one the infinitely rich beds of Devon Island were covered by an impenetrable mud. The oysters perished in their shells.

In time, say a year and a half, the currents of the Choptank would eat away the mud and once more reveal the shelf upon which untold generations of new oysters would flourish. The shells of the dead oysters would be there, gnarled and craggy and inviting to the young spat that would be looking for a ledge to grab hold of. The spat would find a home; the nourishing plankton would drift by; the oyster beds of Devon Island would exist once more, but for the meantime they were obliterated in the silt of the great storm.

Another resident of the Chesapeake was also intensely affected by the hurricane of 1886, but he was better able to cope with the disaster, for he could move, and by taking precautions, adjust to altered circumstances. He was Jimmy, the time-honored Chesapeake name for the male blue crab, that delicious crustacean upon which so much of the wealth of the bay depended.

While the storm still lay off Norfolk, gathering speed and water, Jimmy, resting in the grassy waters at the edge of Turlock Marsh, perceived that a radical change in the atmosphere was about to occur. And it would probably arrive at the worst possible moment for him. How could he know these two facts? He was exceedingly sensitive to changes in atmospheric pressure or to any other factors which affected the waters of the bay. If a storm of unusual force was developing, he would be made aware by the sharp drop in barometric pressure and would prepare to take those protective measures which had rescued him in the past. Also, he knew intuitively when he must climb painfully out of his old shell, which was made of inert matter that could not grow in size as he grew. He had to discard it and prepare himself for the construction of a new shell better fitted to his increased body size. The time for such a moult was at hand.

When the storm broke, and no great body of water fell on the Choptank, Jimmy felt no signals that a crisis was at hand, so he prepared to shed his old shell, an intricate process which might consume as long as four hours of painful wrestling and contortion. But before the moult could begin, he became aware of a frightening change in the bay. The water level was rising. The salinity was diminishing. And when these two phenomena continued, and indeed accelerated, he became uncomfortable.

During any moult, which might take place three or four times a year as he increased in size, he preferred some secure place like the Turlock Marsh, but if it was going to be flooded with fresh water, it could prove a deathtrap rather than a refuge, so he began swimming strongly out toward the deep center of the bay.

A mature crab like Jimmy could swim at a speed of nearly a mile an hour, so he felt safe, but as he cleared Devon Island and was hit by the rush of saltless water, he felt driven to swim with frenetic energy to protect himself. He would not drop dead in the first flush of fresh water, and he could adjust to surprising variations in salinity for brief periods; but to exist in the way for which his body had been constructed, he needed water with a proper salt content.

But moving into the deeper water meant that he would lose the protection of the marsh for his critical moulting. He would have to go through this complex maneuvering out in the bay, where he would be largely defenseless. But he had no other option.

The silt posed no insurmountable problem. It obscured his vision, to be sure, but it did not settle on him or pin him to the bottom, as it did the oysters. He could flip his many legs and swim clear, so that he was not yet in danger at this stage of the flood, but he did sense that he had to swim down toward the ocean to find the salinity necessary to his survival.

These matters assumed little importance in view of the crucial one at hand. Swimming easily to the bottom of the bay, he found a sandy area, a place he would never have considered for a moult in normal times, and there began his gyrations. First he had to break the seal along the edge of his present shell, and he did this by contracting and expanding his body, forcing water through his system and building up a considerable hydraulic pressure that slowly forced the shell apart, not conspicuously, but far enough for the difficult part of the moult to proceed.

Now he began the slow and almost agonizing business of withdrawing his boneless legs from their protective coverings and manipulating them so that they protruded from the slight opening. With wrenching movements he dislodged the main portion of his body, thrusting it toward the opening, which now widened under pressure from the legs. He had no skeleton, of course, so that he could contort and compress his body into whatever shape was most effective, but he did continue to generate hydraulic pressures through various parts of his body so that the shell was forced apart.

Three hours and twenty minutes after he started this bizarre procedure, he swam free of the old shell and was now adrift in the deep waters of the bay, totally without protection. He had no bony structure in any part of his body, no covering thicker than the sheerest tissue paper, no capacity for self-defense except a much-slowed ability to swim. Any fish that chanced to come his way could gobble him at a gulp; if he had been in shallower water, any bird could have taken him. In these fateful hours all he could do was hide.

And yet, even at his most defenseless moment his new armor was beginning to form. Eighty minutes after the moult he would have a paper-thin covering. After three hours he would have the beginning of a solid shell. And in five hours he would be a hard-shelled crab once more, and would remain that way until his next moult.

But as he waited deep in the bay for his new life, the results of the storm continued to make themselves felt, and now the water was so lacking in salt that he felt he must move south. He swam forcefully and with undiverted purpose, keeping to the eastern edge of the bay where the nutritive grasses produced the best plankton, and after a day he sensed the balance of the water to be more nearly normal.

He was not given time to luxuriate in this new-found security of proper water and a solid shell, for urgings of a primordial character were assaulting him, and he forgot his own preoccupations in order to swim among the grasses, looking for sooks which had been by-passed in the earlier mating periods. These overlooked females, on their way south to spend the winter near the entrance of the bay, where fertile sooks traditionally prepared to lay their eggs, sent out frantic signals to whatever males might be in the vicinity, for this was the final period in which they could be fertilized.

Jimmy, probing the marshes, detected such signals and swam with extraordinary energy into the weeds, from which a grateful sook came rushing at him. As soon as she saw that she had succeeded in attracting a male, she became tenderly passive and allowed him to turn her about with his claws and mount her from behind, forming with his many legs a kind of basket in which he would cradle her for the next three days.

This was her time to moult, and Jimmy gave her a protection he had not enjoyed. Covering her completely, he could fend off any fishes that might attack or beat away any birds. Turtles, too, could be avoided and otters that loved to feed on shell-less crabs. For three days he would defend her, holding her gently as she went through her own difficult gyrations of moulting.

When she succeeded in escaping from her old shell, she allowed Jimmy to cast it aside with his feet. She was now completely defenseless, a creature without a skeleton or any bony structure, and at this moment it became possible for the two crabs, he with a shell and she without, to engage in sex, an act which required six or seven hours.

When it was completed he continued to cradle her gently for two days, until her new shell was formed. Only when he felt it secure beneath him did he release her, and then the two crabs separated, she to swim to the lower end of the bay to develop her fertilized eggs, he to the northerly areas to spend the winter in the deeps.

But in 1886 it was not to be as simple as that, for when the Susquehanna broke its banks, flooding the land on either side of the river for a distance of miles, a vicious problem developed: the flood waters upset privies, flushed out septic pools and cleaned out manure dumps, throwing into the swiftly moving waters of the river an incredible accumulation of sewage. In each town that the river inundated on its rampage south, it reamed out the sewage ponds until at the end, when it emptied into the Chesapeake, it was nothing but one mighty cloaca carrying with it enough poisons to contaminate the entire bay.

The effect was worsened by the fact that in the big cities the river picked up huge quantities of industrial waste, especially the newly developed oils, which spread the poisons over the entire surface of the bay. Rarely had the Chesapeake been called upon to absorb such a concentration of lethal agents. It failed.

From the mouth of the river to the mouth of the bay the entire body of water became infected with a dozen new poisons. Those fortunate oysters which managed to escape the silt did not escape the fatal germs, and that October all who ate the few oysters that were caught ran the risk of death, and many died. The bluefish were contaminated and typhoid spread where they were eaten. The crabs were sorely hit, their delicate flesh acting as veritable blotting paper to absorb the germs. In New York and Baltimore families that ate them died.

The fishing industry in the Chesapeake was prostrated, and two years would pass before fresh waters from the Susquehanna and the Rappahannock and the James would flush out the bay and make it once more habitable for oysters and crabs.

Jimmy, seeking refuge at the bottom of the bay, and his impregnated mate, heading south to breed her young, had conducted their mating in an eddy of water heavily infected by the sewage of this vast cesspool, and they, too, died.

The Dogs

THE GOLDEN AGE OF THE EASTERN SHORE CAME IN THAT FOUR-
decade span from 1880 to 1920 when the rest of the nation
allowed the marshy counties to sleep undisturbed. True, in
these years the world experienced panics and wars, and revolutions
and contested elections, but these had almost no impact on the
somnolent estuaries and secluded coves. Roads now connected the
important towns situated at the heads of rivers, but they were nar-
row and dusty, and it took wagons days to cover what a speedy boat
could negotiate in an hour. When roads paved with white oyster
shells did arrive, at the end of this happy age, they were usually one
car-width only and formed not a reasonable means of transportation
but a lively invitation to suicide.

There was, of course, excitement, but it rarely arrived from the
outside world. A black male servant was accused of assaulting a
white woman, and a lynching party composed mainly of Turlocks
and Cavenys broke down the jail to string the accused from an oak
tree, but Judge Hathaway Steed proposed to have no such blot on
his jurisdiction; armed only with a family pistol, he confronted the
mob and ordered it to disperse. The terrified black man was then
transported to a neighboring county, where he was properly hanged.

The Eastern Shore baseball league, composed of six natural
rivals, including Easton, Crisfield, Chestertown and Patamoke,

flourished and became notorious for having produced Home Run Baker, who would hit in one year the unheard-of total of twelve round-trippers. A luxurious ferryboat left Baltimore every Saturday and Sunday at seven-thirty in the morning to transport day-trippers to a slip at Claiborne, where the throngs would leave the ship and crowd into the cars of the Baltimore, Chesapeake and Atlantic Railroad for a two-hour race across the peninsula to Ocean City on the Atlantic. At four forty-five in the afternoon the railroad cars would refill, the train would chug its way back to Claiborne, passengers would reboard the ferry and arrive back at Baltimore at ten-thirty at night—all for one dollar and fifty cents.

One of the adventures which caused most excitement came in 1887 when a ship commanded by Captain Thomas Lightfoot, a troublemaker if there ever was one, docked at Patamoke with its cargo of ice sawed from the fresh-water ponds of Labrador. When the sawdust had been washed away, and the blue-green cakes were stored in icehouses along the riverfront, Captain Lightfoot produced an object which was to cause as much long-lasting trouble as the golden apple that Paris was required to award to the most beautiful goddess.

'I've somethin' extra for you,' Lightfoot announced as he directed one of his black stevedores to fetch the item from below. 'Before it appears I wish to inform you that it is for sale, ten dollars cash.'

A moment later the stevedore appeared on deck leading by a leash one of the most handsome dogs ever seen in Maryland. He was jet-black, sturdy in his front quarters, sleek and powerful in his hind, with a face so intelligent that it seemed he might speak at any moment. His movements were quick, his dark eyes following every development nearby, yet his disposition appeared so equable that he seemed always about to smile.

'He's called a Labrador,' Lightfoot said. 'Finest huntin' dog ever developed.'

'He's what?' Jake Turlock snapped.

'Best huntin' dog known.'

'Can't touch a Chesapeake retriever,' Turlock said, referring to the husky red dog bred especially for bay purposes.

44

'This dog,' said Lightfoot, 'will take your Chesapeake and teach him his ABC's.'

'That dog ain't worth a damn,' Turlock said. 'Too stocky up front.'

But there was something about this new animal that captivated Tim Caveny, whose red Chesapeake had just died without ever fulfilling the promise he had shown as a pup—'Fine in the water and persistent in trackin' downed birds, but not too bright. Downright stupid, if you ask me.' This new black dog displayed a visible intelligence which gave every sign of further development, and Caveny announced, 'I'd like to see him.'

Captain Lightfoot, suspecting that in Caveny he had found his pigeon, turned the Labrador loose, and with an almost psychic understanding that his future lay with this Irishman, the dog ran to Caveny, leaned against his leg and nuzzled his hand.

It was an omen. Tim's heart was lost, and he said, 'I'll take him.'

'Mr. Caveny, you just bought the best Labrador ever bred.' With grandiloquent gestures he turned the animal over to his new owner, and the dog, sensing that he had found a permanent master, stayed close to Tim, and licked his hand and rubbed against him and looked up with dark eyes overflowing with affection.

Tim paid the ten dollars, then reached down and patted his new hunting companion. 'Come on, Lucifer,' he said.

'That's a hell of a name for a dog,' Turlock growled.

'He's black, ain't he?'

'If he's black, call him Nigger.'

'He's Old Testament black,' Tim said. And to Captain Lightfoot's surprise, he recited, ' "How art thou fallen from heaven, O Lucifer, son of the morning!" ' Turning his back on the others, he stooped over the dog, roughed his head and said in a low voice, 'You'll be up in the morning, Lucifer, early, early.'

Lightfoot then startled the crowd by producing three other dogs of this new breed, one male and two females, and these, too, he sold to the hunters of Patamoke, assuring each purchaser, 'They can smell ducks, and they've never been known to lose a cripple.'

'To me they look like horse manure,' Jake Turlock said.

'They what?' Caveny demanded.

'I said,' Turlock repeated, 'that your black dog looks like a horse turd.'

Slowly Tim handed the leash he had been holding to a bystander. Then, with a mighty swipe, he knocked Turlock to the wet and salty boards of the wharf. The waterman stumbled in trying to regain his feet, and while he was off balance Caveny saw a chance to deliver an uppercut which almost knocked him into the water. Never one to allow a fallen foe an even chance, Caveny leaped across the planking and kicked the waterman in his left armpit, lifting him well into the air, but this was a mistake, because when Turlock landed, his hand fell upon some lumber stacked for loading onto Captain Lightfoot's ship, and after he had quickly tested three or four clubs, he found one to his liking, and with it delivered such a blow to the Irishman's head that the new owner of the Labrador staggered back, tried to control his disorganized feet, and fell into the Choptank.

In this way the feud between Tim Caveny, owner of a black Labrador, and Jake Turlock, owner of a red Chesapeake, began.

The first test of the two dogs came in the autumn of 1888 at the dove shoot on the farm of old Lyman Steed, who had spent his long life running one of the Refuge plantations and had now retired to a stretch of land near Patamoke.

Nineteen first-class hunters of the area convened at regular intervals during the dove season to shoot this most interesting of the small game birds: gentlemen like Lyman Steed, middle-class shopkeepers and rough watermen like Jake Turlock and Tim Caveny. For a dove shoot was one of the most republican forms of sport so far devised. Here a man's worth was determined by two criteria: the way he fired his gun and how he managed his dog.

Each hunter was allowed to bring one dog to the shoot, and the animal had to be well trained, because the birds came charging in at low altitude, swerved and dodged in unbelievable confusion and, on the lucky occasions when they were hit, fell maliciously in unpredictable spots. If there was a swamp nearby, as on the Steed farm, the doves would fall there. If there were brambles, the dying doves seemed to seek them out, and the only practical way for the hunter to retrieve his dove, if he hit one, was to have a dog trained to leap forward when he saw a dove fall from the sky and find it no matter where it dropped. The dog must also lift the fallen bird gently in its teeth, carry it without bruising it against thorns, and drop it at the feet of his master. A dove hunt was more a test of dog than of master.

Jake Turlock had a well-trained beast, a large, surly red-haired Chesapeake, specially bred to work the icy waters of the bay in fall and winter. These dogs were unusual in that they grew a double matting of hair and produced an extra supply of oil to lubricate it. They could swim all day, loved to dive into the water for a fallen goose and were particularly skilled in breaking their way through ice. Like most of this breed, Jake's Chesapeake had a vile temper and would allow himself to be worked only by his master. Every other gunner in the field was his enemy and their dogs were beneath his contempt, but he was kept obedient by Jake's stern cry: 'Hey-You, heel!'

His name was Hey-You. Jake had started calling him that when he first arrived at the Turlock shack, a fractious, bounding pup giving no evidence that he could ever be trained. In fact, Jake had thought so little of him that he delayed giving him a proper name. 'Hey-You! Get the dove!' The pup would look quizzical, wait, consider whether he wanted to obey or not, then leap off when Jake kicked him.

So during his useless youth he was plain 'Hey-You, into the water for the goose!' But at the age of three, after many kicks and buffetings, he suddenly developed into a marvelous hunting dog, a raider like his master, a rough-and-tumble, uncivilized beast who seemed made for the Chesapeake. 'Hey-You! Go way down and fetch the dove.' So when this red-haired dog swaggered onto the dove field this October day, he was recognized as one of the best ever trained in the Patamoke area.

Lucifer, Tim Caveny's Labrador, was an unknown quantity, for he had never before participated in a dove shoot; furthermore, he had been trained in a manner quite different from Hey-You. 'My children were raised with love,' the Irishman said, 'and my dog is trained the same way.' From the moment Lucifer came down off Captain Lightfoot's ice ship, he had known nothing but love.

His glossy coat was kept nourished by a daily supply of fat from the Caveny table, and his nails were trimmed. In return he gave the Caveny family his complete affection. 'I believe that dog would lay down his life for me,' Mrs. Caveny told her neighbors, for when she fed him he always looked up at her with his great black eyes and rubbed against her hand. A peddler came to the door one day, unexpectedly and in a frightening manner; Lucifer's hackles rose, and he leaned forward tensely, waiting for a sign. Startled at seeing the man, Mrs. Caveny emitted a short gasp, whereupon Lucifer shot like a thunderbolt for the man's throat.

'Down, Lucifer!' she cried, and he stopped almost in midair.

But whether he could discipline himself to retrieve doves was another matter. Jake Turlock predicted widely, 'The stupid Irishman has spoiled his dog, if'n he was any good to begin with.' Other hunters who had trained their beasts more in the Turlock tradition agreed, adding, 'He ain't gonna get much out of that what-you-call-it—Labrador.'

But Caveny persisted, talking to Lucifer in sweet Irish phrases, trying to convince the dumb animal that great success awaited him on the dove field. 'Luke, you and me will get more doves than this town ever seen. Luke, when I say, "Fetch the dove!" you're to go direct to the spot you think it fell. Then run out in wide and wider circles.' Whether the dog would do this was uncertain, but Tim had tried with all his guile to get the animal in a frame of mind conducive to success. Now, as he led him to Lyman Steed's farm, he prayed that his lessons had been in the right direction, but when he turned the last corner and saw the other eighteen men with their Chesapeakes awaiting him, eager to see what he had accomplished with this strange animal, his heart fluttered and he felt dizzy.

Pulling gently on the rope attached to the dog's collar, he brought him back, kneeled beside him and whispered in his lilting brogue, 'Lucifer, you and me is on trial. They're all watchin' us.'

He stroked the dog's glistening neck and said, 'At my heel constantly, little fellow. You don't move till I fire. And when I do, Luke, for the love of a merciful God, find that dove. Soft mouth, Luke, soft mouth and drop him at my toes, like you did with the rag dolls.'

As if he knew what his master was saying, Luke turned and looked at Tim impatiently, as if to say, 'I know my job. I'm a Labrador.'

The field contained about twenty acres and had recently been harvested, so that it provided a large, flat, completely open area, but it was surrounded by a marsh on one side, a large blackberry bramble on another, and a grove of loblollies covering a thicket of underbrush on a third. The doves would sweep in over the loblollies, drop low, hear gunfire and veer back toward the brambles. Placement of gunners was an art reserved for Judge Hathaway Steed, who hunted in an expensive Harris tweed imported from London.

The judge had been a hunter all his life, raised Chesapeakes and sold them to his friends. He had acquired a much better intuition concerning doves than he had of the law, and he now proposed to place his eighteen subordinates strategically, about sixty yards apart and in a pattern which pretty well covered the perimeter of the field. Toward the end of his assignments he came to Tim Caveny. 'You there, with the what-you-call-it dog.'

'Labrador,' Caveny said, tipping his hat respectfully, as his father had done in the old country when the laird spoke.

'Since we can't be sure a dog like that can hunt . . .'

'He can hunt.'

The judge ignored this. 'Take that corner,' he said, and Tim wanted to complain that doves rarely came to that corner, but since he was on trial he kept his mouth shut, but he was most unhappy when he saw Jake Turlock receive one of the best positions.

Then everyone stopped talking, for down the road edging the field came a carriage driven by a black man. On the seat beside him sat a very old gentleman with a shotgun across his knees. This was Lyman Steed, owner of the field. He was eighty-seven years old and so frail that a stranger would have wondered how he could lift a gun, let alone shoot it. Behind him, eyes and ears alert, rode a large red Chesapeake.

The carriage came to a halt close to where Hathaway Steed was allocating the spots, and the black driver descended, unfolded a canvas chair and lifted the old man down into it. 'Where do we sit today?' Steed asked in a high, quavering voice.

'Take him over by the big tree,' Hathaway said, and the black man carried the chair and its contents to the spot indicated. There he scraped the ground with his foot, making a level platform, and on it he placed the owner of the farm and one of the best shots in this meet. 'We's ready,' the black man cried, and the judge gave his last instructions: 'If you see a dove that the men near you don't, call "Mark!" Keep your dogs under control. And if the dove flies low, absolutely no shooting in the direction of the man left or right.'

The men took their positions. It was half after one in the afternoon. The sun was high and warm; insects droned. The dogs were restless, but each stayed close to his master, and the men wondered whether there would be any doves, because on some days they failed to show.

But not today. From the woods came six doves, flying low in their wonderfully staggered pattern, now in this direction, now swooping in that. Jake Turlock, taken by surprise, fired and hit nothing. 'Mark!' he shouted at the top of his voice. Tim Caveny fired and hit nothing. 'Mark!' he bellowed. In swift, darting patterns the doves dived and swirled and twisted, and three other hunters fired at them, to no avail, but as the birds tried to leave the field old Lyman Steed had his gun waiting. With a splendid shot he hit his target, and his big Chesapeake leaped out before the bird hit the ground and retrieved it before the dove could even flutter. Bearing it proudly in his mouth, but not touching its flesh with his teeth, he trotted back, head high, to his master and laid the bird at the old man's feet.

'That's how it's done,' Tim Caveny whispered to his Labrador.

There was a long wait and the hunters began to wonder if they

would see any more doves, but Hathaway Steed, walking the rounds to police the action, assured each man as he passed, 'We're going to see flocks.'

He was right. At about two-thirty they started coming in. 'Mark!' one hunter shouted as they passed him before he could fire. Jake Turlock was waiting and knocked one down, whereupon Hey-You leaped out into the open field, pounced on the fallen bird and brought it proudly back. Jake looked at Tim, but the Irishman kept his eyes on the sky. He did whisper to Lucifer, 'Any dog can retrieve in an open field. Wait till one falls in the brambles.'

On the next flight Tim got no chance to shoot, but Turlock did, and this time he hit a bird that had come over the field, heard the shooting and doubled back. This dove fell into brambles. 'Fetch the dove!' Jake told his Chesapeake, but the bushes were too thick. That bird was lost.

But now another dove flew into Tim's range, and when he fired, this one also fell into brambles. 'Fetch the dove!' Tim said calmly, his heart aching for a good retrieve.

Lucifer plunged directly for the fallen bird but could not penetrate the thick and thorny briars. Unlike Turlock's Chesapeake, he did not quit, for he heard his master calling softly, 'Circle, Luke! Circle!' And he ran in wide circles until he found a back path to the brambles. But again he was stopped, and again his master cried, 'Circle, Luke!' And this time he found an entrance which allowed him to roam freely, but with so much ranging he had lost an accurate guide to the fallen bird. Still he heard his master's voice imploring, 'Circle, Luke!' and he knew that this meant he still had a chance.

So in the depth of the bramble patch, but below the reach of the thorns, he ran and scrambled and clawed and finally came upon Caveny's bird. He gave a quiet *yup,* and when Tim heard this his heart expanded. Lucifer had passed his first big test, but on the way out of the patch the dog smelled another fallen bird, Turlock's, and he brought this one too.

When he laid the two doves at Tim's feet, the Irishman wanted to kneel and kiss his rough black head, but he knew that all the

hunters in his area were watching, so in a manly way he patted the dog, then prepared for his moment of triumph.

It was a custom in dove shooting that if a hunter downed a bird which his dog could not retrieve and another man's dog did fetch it, the second hunter was obligated to deliver the dove to the man who had downed it. It was a nice tradition, for it allowed the second man to make a show of carrying the dove to its rightful owner while all the other hunters observed his act of sportsmanship. Implied in the gesture was the challenge: 'My dog can retrieve and yours can't.'

Proudly Tim Caveny walked the hundred-odd yards to where Jake Turlock was standing. Lucifer started to follow, but Tim cried sharply, 'Stay!' and the dog obeyed. The other hunters took note of this, then watched as Tim gravely delivered the bird, but at this moment another hunter shouted, 'Mark!' and a whole covey flew over.

Automatically Jake and Tim fired, and two birds fell. Jake's Hey-You was on the spot, of course, and proudly ran out to recover the dove his master had knocked down, but Lucifer was far distant from where his master had shot, yet he was so obedient to the earlier command, 'Stay,' that he did not move. But when Tim yelled, 'Fetch the dove,' he leaped off his spot, rushed directly to the fallen bird, and carried it not to where Tim was standing, but back to his assigned location.

The hunter next to Tim on the down side of the field called, 'You got yourself a dog, Tim.'

When Caveny returned to his location and saw the dove neatly laid beside his pouch, he desperately wanted to smother the dark beast with his affection; instead he said merely, 'Good dog, Luke.'

'Mark!' came the call and up went the guns.

The day was a triumph. Luke hunted in marshland as well as he had in brambles. He proved he had a soft mouth. He circled well in woods, and on the open field he was superb. And with it all he displayed the bland, sweet disposition of the Labradors and the Cavenys.

It was the tradition on these dove shoots for one member at the end of the day to provide refreshments. At quarter to five, religiously, the hunting ceased. The dogs were put back on leashes, and if the owners had come by wagon, were stowed in back while their masters ate cold duck and drank Baltimore beer. Turlock and Caveny, having come on foot, tied their dogs to trees, and as they did so the former muttered, 'Doves ain't nothin', Caveny. It's what a dog does in ice that counts.'

'Lucifer will handle ice,' Tim said confidently.

'On the bay proper, my Chesapeake is gonna eat 'im up. Out there they got waves.'

'Your Labrador looks like a breed to be proud of,' old Lyman Steed said as the black servant carried him into position to share the duck.

'Possibilities,' Judge Hathaway Steed said. 'But we won't know till we see him after geese.'

Each man complimented Tim on what he had accomplished with this strange dog, but each also predicted, 'Probably won't be much on the bay. Hair's not thick enough.'

Tim did not argue, but when he got Lucifer home he hugged him and gave him chicken livers, and whispered, 'Lucifer, geese is just doves, grown bigger. You'll love the water, cold or not.' During the whole dove season, during which this fine black dog excelled, Tim repeated his assurances: 'You're gonna do the same with geese.'

The test came in November. As the four men and their dogs holed up in a blind at the Turlock marshes, Jake reminded them, 'Geese ain't so plentiful now. Can't afford any mistakes, man or dog.' He was right. Once the Choptank and its sister rivers had been home for a million geese; now the population had diminished to less than four hundred thousand, and bagging them became more difficult. Jake, a master of the goose call, tried from dawn till ten in the morning to lure the big birds down, but failed. The hunters had a meager lunch, and toward dusk, when it seemed that the day was a failure, nine geese wheeled in, lowered the pitch of their wings, spread their feet and came right at the blind. Guns blazed, and before the smoke had cleared, Jake's Chesapeake had leaped out of the blind and with powerful swimming motions had retrieved the goose that his master had appeared to kill. Lucifer went into the water, too, but many seconds after Hey-You, and he was both splashy and noisy in making his retrieve of Tim's goose.

'Sure doesn't like cold water,' Jake said contemptuously.

'Neither did yours, when he started,' Tim said.

'A Chesapeake is born lovin' water, colder the better.'

It became obvious to the hunters, after eight mornings in the blind, that while Tim Caveny's new dog was exceptional with doves on warm days, he left much to be desired as a real hunter in the only form of the sport that mattered—goose on water. He displayed a discernible reluctance to plunge into cold waves, and they began to wonder whether he would go into ice at all.

Talk at the store centered on his deficiencies: 'This here Labrador is too soft. Can't hold a candle to a Chesapeake for hard work when it matters. You ask me, I think Caveny bought hisse'f a loser.' Some hunters told him this to his face.

Tim listened and said nothing. In his lifetime he had had four major dogs, all of them Chesapeakes, and he understood the breed almost as well as Jake Turlock did, but he had never owned a dog with the charm of Lucifer, the warmth, the love, and that meant something—'I come home, the room's bigger when that dog's in it.'

'Point is,' the men argued, 'a huntin' dog oughtn't to be in a room in the first place. His job is outside.'

'You don't know Lucifer. Besides, he's sired the best lot of pups in the region. This breed is bound to catch on.'

The Patamoke hunters were a suspicious clan. The most important thing in their lives, more important than wife or church or political party, was the totality of the hunting season: 'You got to have the right gun, the right mates, the right spot, the right eye for the target and, above all, the right dog. And frankly, I doubt the Labrador.' The pups did not sell.

Tim had faith. He talked with Lucifer constantly, encouraging him to leap more quickly into the cold water. He showed what ice was like, and how the dog must break it with his forepaws to make a path for himself to the downed goose. Using every training trick the Choptank had ever heard of, he tried to bring this handsome dog along step by step.

He failed. In January, when real ice formed along the edges of the river, the men went hunting along the banks of the bay itself, and when Jake Turlock knocked down a beautiful goose, it fell on ice about two hundred yards from the blind—'Hey-You, get the bird!'

And the big Chesapeake showed what a marvelous breed he was by leaping into the free water, swimming swiftly to the edge of the ice, then breaking a way for himself right to the goose. Clutching the big bird proudly in his jaws, he plunged back into the icy water, pushed aside the frozen chunks and returned to the blind, entering it with a mighty, water-spraying leap.

'That's what I call a dog,' Jake said proudly, and the men agreed.

Lucifer did not perform so well. He retrieved his goose all right, but hesitantly and almost with protest. He didn't want to leap into the water in the first place; he was not adept at breaking ice; and when he returned to the blind, he ran along the ice for as long as possible before going back into the freezing water.

'He did get the goose,' Jake admitted condescendingly, and for the rest of that long day on the Chesapeake the two dogs performed in this way, with Hey-You doing as well as a water dog could and Lucifer just getting by.

Tim never spoke a harsh word. Lucifer was his dog, a splendid, loving, responsive animal, and if he didn't like cold water, that was a matter between him and his master. And toward dusk the dog found an opportunity to repay Tim's confidence. Jake had shot a big goose, which had fallen into a brambled sort of marsh from which Hey-You could not extract it. The dog tried, swam most valiantly in various directions, but achieved nothing.

In the meantime Lucifer remained in the blind, trembling with eagerness, and Tim realized that his Labrador knew where that goose was. After Hey-You had returned with nothing. Tim said softly, 'Luke, there's a bird out there. Show them how to get it.'

Like a flash the black dog leaped into the water, splashed his way through the semi-ice into the rushy area—and found nothing. 'Luke!' Tim bellowed. 'Circle. Circle!' So the dog ran and splashed and swam in noisy circles and still found nothing, but he would not quit, for his master kept pleading, 'Luke, circle!'

And then he found the goose, grabbed it in his gentle mouth and swam proudly back to the blind. As he was about to place the goose at Tim's feet, the Irishman said quietly, 'No!' And the dog was so attentive to his master that he froze, wanting to know what he had done wrong.

'Over there,' Tim said, and Luke took the goose to Jake, placing it at his feet.

The Gun

THE FEUD BETWEEN THE TWO WATERMEN CONTINUED. THE MEN at the store fired it with unkind comments about Lucifer's deficiencies, but once or twice Caveny caught a hint that their animosity was weakening, for at some unexpected moment a man would see in Tim's dog a quality which made him catch his breath. Outwardly every hunter would growl, 'I want my dog to be rough and able to stand the weather and ready to leap at anyone attackin' me,' but inwardly he would also want the dog to love him. And the way in which Lucifer stayed close to Tim, anxious to detect every nuance in the Irishman's mood, tantalized the men at the store. All they would grant openly was, 'Maybe Tim's got somethin' in that black dog.' But Jake Turlock would not admit even that. 'What he's got is a good lap dog, and that's about it. As for me, I'm interested solely in huntin'.'

Aside from this disagreement over dogs, and a fistfight now and then, the two watermen maintained a warm friendship. They hunted together, fished together and worked the oyster beds in season. But it was the big gun that cemented their partnership, giving it substance and allowing it to blossom.

In these decades when the Eastern Shore flourished, the city of Baltimore also flourished. Some discriminating critics considered it the best city in America, combining the new wealth of the North with the old gentility of the South. The city offered additional rewards: a host of German settlers who gave it intellectual distinction; numerous Italians who gave it warmth. But for most observers, its true excellence derived from the manner in which its hotels and restaurants maintained a tradition of savory cooking: southern dishes, northern meats, Italian spices and German beer.

In 1888 the noblest hotel of them all had opened, the Rennert, eight stories high, with an additional three stories to provide a dome at one end, a lofty belvedere at the other. It was a grand hostelry which boasted, 'Our cooks are Negro. Our waiters wear white gloves.' From the day of its opening, it became noted for the luxuriance of its cuisine: 'Eighteen kinds of game. Fourteen ways to serve oysters. And the best wild duck in America.' To dine at the Rennert was to share the finest the Chesapeake could provide.

Jake Turlock and Tim Caveny had never seen the new hotel, but it was to play a major role in their lives. Its black chefs demanded the freshest oysters, and these were delivered daily during the season by Choptank watermen who packed their catch in burlap bags, speeding them across the bay by special boat. When the boat was loaded with oysters, its principal cargo, the captain could usually find space on deck for a few last-minute barrels crammed with ducks: mallards, redheads, canvasbacks and, the juciest of all, the black. It was in the providing of these ducks for the Rennert that Jake and Tim began to acquire a little extra money, which they saved for the larger project they had in mind.

One night at the store, after arguing about the comparative merits of their dogs, Jake said, 'I know me a man's got a long gun he might want to dispose of.'

Caveny was excited. 'If you can get the gun, I can get me a couple of skiffs.'

Turlock replied, 'Suppose we get the gun and the skiffs, I know me a captain who'll ferry our ducks to the Rennert. Top dollar.'

Caveny completed the self-mesmerization by adding, 'We put aside enough money, we can get Paxmore to build us our own boat. Then we're in business.'

So the feuding pair sailed upriver to the landing of a farm owned

by an old man named Greef Twombly, and there they proposi-
tioned him: 'You ain't gonna have much more use for your long
gun, Greef. We aim to buy it.'

'What you gonna use for money?' the toothless old fellow asked.

'We're gonna give you ten dollars cash, which Tim Caveny has
in his pocket right now, and another forty when we start collectin'
ducks.'

'Barrel of that gun was made from special forged iron. My grandfather brought it from London, sixty-two years ago.'

'It's been used.'

'More valuable now than when he got it home.'

'We'll give you sixty.'

'Sixty-five and I'll think about it.'

'Sixty-five it is, and we get possession now.'

Twombly rocked back and forth, considering aspects of the deal,
then led them to one of the proudest guns ever to sweep the ice at
midnight. It was a monstrous affair, eleven feet six inches long,

about a hundred and ten pounds in weight, with a massive stock that could not possibly fit into a man's shoulder, which was good, because if anyone tried to hold this cannon when it fired, the recoil would tear his arm away.

'You ever fire one of these?' the old man asked.

'No, but I've heard,' Turlock said.

'Hearin' ain't enough, son. You charge it with three quarters of a pound of black powder in here, no less, or she won't carry. Then you pour in a pound and a half of Number Six shot, plus one fistful. You tamp her down with greasy wadding, like this, and you're ready. Trigger's kept real tight so you can't explode the charge by accident, because if you did, it would rip the side off'n a house.'

The two watermen admired the huge barrel, the sturdy fittings and the massive oak stock; as they inspected their purchase the old man said, 'You know how to fit her into a skiff?'

'I've seen,' Turlock said.

But Twombly wanted to be sure these new men understood the full complexity of this powerful gun, so he asked them to carry it to the landing, where he had a fourteen-foot skiff with extremely pointed bow and almost no deadrise, chocks occupying what normally would have been the main seat and a curious burlap contraption built into the stern area.

Deftly the old hunter let himself down into the skiff, kneeling in the stern. He then produced a double-ended paddle like the ones Eskimos used, and also two extremely short-handled single paddles. Adjusting his weight and testing the double paddle, he told Jake, 'You can hand her down.'

When the two watermen struggled with the preposterous weight of the gun, the old man said, 'It ain't for boys.' He accepted the gun into the skiff, dropped its barrel between the chocks, flipped a wooden lock, which secured it, then fitted the heavy butt into a socket made of burlap bagging filled with pine needles.

'What you do,' Twombly said, 'is use your big paddle to ease you into position, but when you come close to the ducks you stow it and take out your two hand paddles, like this.' And with the two paddles that looked like whisk brooms, he silently moved the skiff about.

'When you get her into position, you lie on your belly, keep the hand paddles close by and sight along the barrel of the gun. You don't point the gun; you point the skiff. And when you get seventy, eighty ducks in range, you put a lot of pressure on this trigger and—'

The gun exploded with a power that seemed to tear a hole in the sky. The kickback came close to ripping out the stern of the skiff, but the pine needles absorbed it, while a veritable cloud of black smoke curled upward.

'First time I ever shot that gun in daylight,' the old man said. 'It's a killer.'

'You'll sell?'

'You're Lafe Turlock's grandson, ain't you?'

'I am.'

'I had a high regard for Lafe. He could track niggers with the best. Gun's yourn.'

'You'll get your fifty-five,' Jake promised.

'I better,' the old man said ominously.

Caveny produced the two skiffs he had promised, and their mode of operation became standardized: as dusk approached, Jake would inspect his skiff to be sure he had enough pine needles in the burlap to absorb the recoil; he also cleaned the huge gun, prepared his powder, checked his supply of shot; Tim in the meantime was preparing his own skiff and feeding the two dogs.

Hey-You ate like a pig, gulping down whatever Caveny produced, but Lucifer was more finicky; there were certain things, like chicken guts, he would not eat. But the two animals had learned to exist together, each with his own bowl, growling with menace if the other approached. They had never engaged in a real fight; Hey-You would probably have killed Lucifer had one been joined, but they did nip at each other and a kind of respectful discipline was maintained.

Whenever they saw Jake oiling the gun, they became tense, would not sleep and spied on every action of their masters. As soon as it became clear that there was to be duck hunting, they bounded with joy and kept close to the skiff in which Caveny would take them onto the water.

Duck hunting with a big gun was an exacting science best performed in the coldest part of winter with no moon, for then the watermen enjoyed various advantages; they could cover the major part of their journey by sliding their skiffs across the ice; when they reached areas of open water they would find the ducks clustered in great rafts; and the lack of moonlight enabled them to move close without being seen. The tactic required utmost silence; even the crunch of a shoe on frost would spook the ducks. The dogs especially had to remain silent, perched in Caveny's skiff, peering into the night.

When the two skiffs reached open water, about one o'clock in the morning with the temperature at twelve degrees, Tim kept a close watch on the necks of the two dogs; almost always the first indication he had that ducks were in the vicinity came when the hackles rose on Hey-You. He was so attuned to the bay that one night Tim conceded graciously, 'Jake, your dog can see ducks at a hundred yards in pitch-black,' and Turlock replied, 'That's why he's a huntin' dog, not a lap dog . . . like some I know.'

When the ducks were located, vast collections huddling in the cold, Turlock took command. Easing his skiff into the icy water, he adjusted his double-ended paddle, stayed on his knees to keep the center of gravity low, and edged toward the restive fowl. Sometimes it took him an hour to cover a quarter of a mile; he kept the barrel of his gun smeared with lamp black to prevent its reflecting such light as there might be, and in cold darkness he inched forward.

Now he discarded his two-handed paddle and lay flat on his belly, his cheek alongside the stock of the great gun, his hands working the short paddles. It was a time of tension, for the slightest swerve or noise would alert the ducks and they would be off.

Slowly, slowly he began to point the nose of the skiff at the heart of the congregation, and when he had satisfied himself that the muzzle of the gun was pointed in the right direction, he brought his short paddles in and took a series of deep breaths. Then, with his cheek close to the stock but not touching it, and his right hand at the trigger, he extended his forefinger, grasped the heavy trigger —and waited. Slowly the skiff would drift and steady, and when everything was in line, he pulled the trigger.

He was never prepared for the magnitude of the explosion that ripped through the night. It was monstrous, like the fire of a cannon, but in the brief flash it produced he could always see ducks being blown out of the water as if a hundred expert gunners had fired at them.

Now Caveny became the focus. Paddling furiously, he sped his skiff through the dark water, his two dogs quivering with desire to leap into the waves to retrieve the ducks. But he wanted to bring them much closer to where the birds lay, and to do so he enforced a stern discipline. 'No! No!'—that was all he said, but the two dogs obeyed, standing on their hind feet, their forepaws resting on the deadrise like twin figureheads, one red, one black.

'Fetch!' he shouted, and the dogs leaped into the water and began their task of hauling the ducks to the two skiffs, Hey-You always going to Turlock's and Lucifer to Caveny's.

Since Tim's job was to man his shotgun and knock down cripples, he was often too busy to bother with his dog, so the Labrador had perfected a tactic whereby he paddled extra hard with his hind legs, reared out of the water and tossed his ducks into the skiff.

In this way the two watermen, with one explosion of their big gun, sometimes got themselves as many as sixty canvasbacks, ten or twelve blacks and a score of others. On rare occasions they would be able to fire twice in one night, and then their profit was amazing.

As soon as the two skiffs reached Patamoke, the watermen packed their catch in ventilated barrels, which they lined up on the wharf. There they purchased from other night gunners enough additional ducks to make full barrels, which they handed over to the captain of the boat running oysters to the Rennert, and at the end of each month they received from the hotel a check for their services.

Night after night Jake and Tim lurked at the edge of the ice, waiting for the ducks to raft up so that the gun could be fired, and as the barrels filled with canvasbacks and mallards, so their pockets filled with dollars, and they began to think seriously about acquiring a real boat in which they could branch out.

'There's a man on Deal Island, got hisse'f a new kind of boat,' Turlock said one morning as they were packing their ducks.

'What's special?'

'Claims it's the best type ever built for the Chesapeake. Made especially for drudgin'.'

Time out of mind, watermen of the Chesapeake had used two words with unique pronunciation. There was no such thing as an oyster, never had been. It was an arster, and to call it anything else was profanation. And a man did not dredge for arsters, he drudged them. Jake and Tim proposed to become arster drudgers, and the boat they had in mind was ideal for their purpose.

It put in to Patamoke one day, and Turlock ran to the Paxmore Boatyard and asked Gerrit Paxmore to join him in inspecting it. 'This is quite remarkable,' the Quaker said. And he began to analyze what the Deal Island men had done.

'Very shallow draft, so it can go anywhere on the flats. Single mast far forward, but look how it's raked! Gives them a triangular sail. More room on deck. Also allows the tip of the mast to hang over the hold, so that they can drop a line and haul cargo out. Enormous boom to give them drudging power. Very low freeboard, so they won't have to hoist the arsters too far, and it looks like it could sleep six.'

But then his practiced eye saw something he definitely did not like. 'She has no protruding keel, which accounts for her shallow draft, but she does have a retractable centerboard. I don't like that, not at all.'

'She has to have,' Turlock said. 'To counterbalance the sail.'

'I know, but to insert a centerboard, you've got to penetrate the keel.'

'What's the fault in that?'

'At Paxmore's we never touch the keel.' He looked at an old boat tied to the wharf, its backbone hogged. 'Our boats don't do that.'

He would not discuss the new craft any further, but returned to his yard; Turlock, however, asked the captain if he could serve on the next oystering, and the Deal Island man said, 'Come aboard,' so Jake dredged for six days, and when he came ashore he told Caveny, 'That's the finest boat's ever been built. It helps you work.'

So they went back to Paxmore, and Tim listened as his partner extolled the new craft. 'Mr. Paxmore, that boat helps you drudge. You can feel that huge boom bendin' to the job.'

But Paxmore was adamant. 'I would never feel comfortable, building a boat whose keel had been half-severed.'

'Suppose you don't feel comfortable? How about us? We're buyin' the boat.'

'I build by my own principles,' Paxmore said. 'If someone else can use my boat when she's built, good. If not, I'm ready to wait till the proper buyer comes along.'

Jake stepped back, looked at the self-satisfied Quaker and said, 'You'll go out of business in six months.'

'We're in our third century,' Paxmore said, and he would not discuss boatbuilding any further.

As a matter of fact, the question almost became academic one wintry February night when the two watermen had crept out to a spacious lagoon in the ice; there must have been three thousand ducks rafted there beneath a frozen late-rising moon. Caveny became aware of how cold it was when Lucifer left his spot on the gunwale and huddled in the bottom of the skiff. Hey-You turned twice to look at his cowardly companion, then moved to the middle of the bow as if obliged to do the work of two.

Jake, seeing this tremendous target before him—more ducks in one spot than they had ever found before—decided that he would use not a pound and a half of shot but almost twice that much. 'I'll rip a tunnel through the universe of ducks.' But to propel such a heavy load he required an extra-heavy charge, so into the monstrous gun he poured more than a pound of black powder. He also rammed home a double wadding. 'This is gonna be a shot to remember. Rennert's will owe us enough money to pay for our boat.'

Cautiously he moved his lethal skiff into position, waited, took a deep breath and pulled the trigger.

'*Whoooom!*' The gun produced a flash that could have been seen

for miles and a bang that reverberated across the bay. The tremendous load of shot slaughtered more than a hundred and ten ducks and seven geese. It also burst out the back of Jake's skiff, knocked him unconscious and threw him a good twenty yards aft into the dark and icy waters.

The next minutes were a nightmare. Caveny, having seen his partner fly through the air during the brief flash of the explosion, started immediately to paddle in the direction of where the body might fall, but the two dogs, trained during their entire lives to retrieve fallen birds, found themselves involved with the greatest fall of ducks they had ever encountered, and they refused to bother with a missing man.

'Goddamnit!' Caveny yelled. 'Leave them ducks alone and find Jake.'

But the dogs knew better. Back and forth they swam on their joyous mission, gathering ducks at a rate they had never imagined in their twitching dreams.

'Jake! Where in hell are you?'

In the icy darkness he could find no way of locating the drowning man; all he knew was the general direction of Jake's flight, and now, in some desperation, he began sweeping the area—with almost no chance of finding his mate.

But then Lucifer swam noisily to the skiff, almost reprimanding Tim for having moved it away from the fallen ducks, and after he had thrown two ducks into the skiff, he swam casually a few yards, grabbed the unconscious and sinking Turlock by an arm, hauled him to the skiff, and returned quickly to the remaining ducks.

When Tim finally succeeded in dragging Jake aboard, he could think of nothing better to do than to slap the unconscious man's face with his icy glove, and after a few minutes Jake revived. Bleary-eyed, he tried to determine where he was, and when at last he perceived that he was in Caveny's skiff and not his own, he bellowed, 'What have you done with the gun?'

'I been savin' you!' Tim yelled back, distraught by this whole affair and by the mangled ducks that kept piling into his skiff.

'To hell with me. Save the gun!'

So now the two watermen began paddling furiously and with no plan, trying to locate the other skiff, and after much fruitless effort Jake had the brains to shout, 'Hey-You! Where are you?'

And from a direction they could not have anticipated, a dog barked, and when they paddled there they found a sorely damaged skiff almost sinking from the weight of its big gun and the many ducks Hey-You had fetched.

On the doleful yet triumphant return to Patamoke, Tim Caveny could not resist pointing out that it had been his Labrador who had saved Turlock's life, but Jake growled through the ice festooning his chin, 'Granted, but it was Hey-You that saved the gun, and that's what's important.'

The Skipjacks

THE PARTNERS NOW HAD ENOUGH MONEY FOR A SERIOUS DOWN payment on an oyster dredger, but before they made a contract with any boatbuilder, Jake wanted Tim to sail aboard one of the Deal Island innovations, so they shipped with a mean-spirited gentleman from that island, and Tim came home convinced that no boat but one of that type would satisfy him.

But he had also learned that the best boats on the bay were those built by Paxmore's, always had been, and he was not willing to settle for second-best. He therefore launched a campaign to convince his partner that they must do business with the Quaker, no matter what his idiosyncrasies. 'Let him build the boat however he wants. He'll do it right.'

Jake was obdurate. 'The three boats I seen are just what we want. I won't have no details sacrificed to any square-headed Quaker thinks he can improve the breed.'

For a week the two watermen could not even agree to take their big gun out for ducks, and no barrels were shipped to the Rennert. Then Tim counted their savings, concluded that it was safe to go ahead, and reluctantly agreed that since Paxmore refused to make what they wanted, they must give their commission to some other builder. Tim was not happy with this decision but was prepared to go ahead with it. And then one morning, as they argued as to

which of the alternative builders they would employ, a boy came with news that Mr. Paxmore wanted to see them.

It was a strange but very Choptank trio that convened. Gerrit Paxmore was the youngest of the three—stiff, wearing black shoes, heavy black trousers and waistcoat. He suffered from a forbidding countenance that rarely broke into a smile, and he spoke precisely, as if recording every word against some possible future challenge, at which time he would be prepared not only to explain it but to fulfill it. Patrons soon discovered that to do business with Paxmore was not easy, but it was reassuring.

Jake Turlock had his family's leanness, height and sour visage. He wore run-over shoes, baggy trousers, torn shirt and smashed hat, items which he rarely changed. He could read and write, having been well taught by the first Caveny from Ireland, but he posed as an illiterate. He hated Negroes and Catholics but found himself consistently thrown in with them, and much to his surprise, liked the individuals with whom he worked. He was, for example, convinced that Tim Caveny, as a Papist, was an insidious type, but he had never discovered any other man with whom it was so comforting to work. Tim had forced him to save money; had saved his life when the big gun blew out the back of the skiff; and up to now had proved reliable in emergencies. But Jake felt certain that when a real crunch came, Caveny would be found wanting.

Tim was much like his father, old Michael, the schoolteacher of indomitable optimism. He was inclined to be pudgy, lazy and preposterous. He loved his church and his family; but he loved even more the concept of sticking everlastingly to the job at hand. He was, in his own way, as much a puritan as Gerrit Paxmore, which was why these two men understood each other. Tim was invariably willing to bet his money that *his* nigger would outfight the other, that *his* dog would retrieve more doves, that *his* boat would outsail any other on the bay. He existed in a world of perpetual challenge, in which he constantly faced men who were bigger than he or had more money. But since he was Irish, a reliable margin of good luck hung over him like an aura. He strove for the best, and the best sometimes happened.

It was he who opened the conversation that morning. 'Mr. Paxmore, we've decided—'

'We've decided nothin',' Turlock interrupted.

'Perhaps I can assist thee,' Paxmore said gently. 'I've consulted with my men, and we want to try our hands at one of these new boats. What does thee call them?'

'Skipjack,' Turlock said.

'After the fish that skips over the water,' Tim interposed. 'And it does, Mr. Paxmore. This boat skims.'

'So we've decided, here at Paxmore's . . .' He coughed, placed his hands on the desk as if confessing all, and said, 'We'll build thy boat.'

'Centerboard in position?' Turlock asked.

'Of course.'

'How much?' Caveny asked.

''We think we can do it . . .' With almost a visible shudder he looked at the two supplicants, who could not possibly have the money required, then said in a whisper, 'We could do it for twelve hundred dollars.'

As soon as the words were uttered, Tim Caveny slapped down a bundle of bills. 'We can pay five hundred and forty dollars on deposit.'

This was more than twice what Paxmore had expected, and with an astonishment he could not control he asked, 'Where did thee acquire so much?' and Caveny said, like a fellow industrialist, 'We've been savin' it.'

Jake Turlock hated to surrender cash. 'Would it be cheaper, Mr. Paxmore, if me and Tim was to provide you with your timber?'

'It would indeed!'

'How much cheaper?'

'Thee would include keel, mast, boom?'

'You give us the length. We have the trees.'

Paxmore studied a paper which betrayed the fact that he wanted to build this boat no matter what the profit: he had a complete sketch of an improved skipjack, waiting to be transformed into a sleek bay craft. 'Mast, at least sixty-five feet tall, two feet in diameter at the thirty-foot mark, to allow for trimming.'

'I have my eye on just the tree,' Jake said.

'Boom fifty-three feet.'

'That's awful long for a boom. Longer than the boat itself.'

'That's the design. Bowsprit a good twenty-two feet.'

'She's gonna be very top-heavy, with those dimensions,' Turlock said.

'She'll be ballasted,' Paxmore assured him, but he had not yet said how much reduction he would allow if Turlock cut the timber from the woods behind his marsh.

'The savin's?' Jake asked.

'Thee will save three hundred and fifty dollars.'

'Tim,' the waterman said, 'get us some axes.'

The work the two men did in the ensuing weeks was awesome, for not only did they chop down oaks and loblollies during the day; they also took their long gun out each night, because only by constantly supplying the Rennert with barrels of ducks could they discharge the remaining debt on the skipjack. In addition to all this,

Tim Caveny, in any spare moments, was constructing something that was about to shock the bay.

He worked in secret with his oldest boy, hammering at pipes, spending hours at a forge in town. The only indication Jake caught that his partner was up to something came one dawn when he helped lift mallards and canvasbacks from Tim's skiff. 'What you doin' with them extra struts?'

'I got me an idea,' the Irishman said, but he confided nothing.

And then one night as the watermen went down to their skiffs, Caveny revealed his masterpiece. From the front of his boat protruded not one but seven guns, each with a barrel two inches in diameter. They fanned out like the tail of a turkey gobbler, coming together where the triggers would normally be. There were no triggers. 'That's my invention. What we do is load the seven guns—powder, pellets and tampin', all in order.'

'How you gonna fire 'em?' Jake asked.

'Ah ha! See this little iron trough?'

Jake had seen it, and had wondered what purpose it served; he could not have anticipated the insane proposal that Tim now made.

'The trough fits in here, just below the powder entrances to the seven guns. We fill it with powder all the way acrost. At this end, we light it. Whoosh! It fires each of the seven guns in order, and we kill so many ducks we're gonna need two extra skiffs.'

'It'll backfire and scorch you to death,' Jake predicted.

'It ain't yet.'

'You mean you fired this battery?'

'Three times. And tonight we fire it at the biggest mess o' ducks we can find.'

They paddled down the center of the Choptank, seeking a strong field of ice across which they could push their arsenal. North of Devon Island, where the rivers penetrating inland clustered, they found some, pulled their skiffs onto it and started the long, patient movement inland. Hey-You and Lucifer, each in his own skiff, made no noise, and when the hunters reached open water, everyone remained quiet for about half an hour, adjusting eyes to the darkness and allowing whatever birds lurked ahead to quieten.

Hey-You's hackles rose, and Tim whispered, 'It's a congregation!'

'We'll move together,' Jake proposed.

'But I'm to shoot first,' Tim said.

'Damned right. I'll be there to catch you when it blows you apart.'

The plan was for Tim to ignite his powder trough and, at the explosion of the first gun, for Jake to fire his monster. They calculated that Tim's seven guns backed up by Jake's would fire so nearly simultaneously that a curtain of lead would be thrown across the bay; few fowl would escape.

Each man eased himself into his skiff, instructed his dog where to sit, and started to work the small hand paddles. One could barely see the other, but an occasional hand signal indicated the preferred course, and slowly they approached the resting ducks. There were so many that Tim could not even estimate their number; all he knew was that they presented a worthy target.

As the time for lighting his powder train approached he muttered a brief prayer: 'Dearest God who protects watermen, don't let nothin' spook 'em.'

The ducks slept. The two skiffs moved silently into position. The dogs sat with every muscle tensed. And the men lay prone, their faces close to their guns. There was no moon, no snow.

Gently, but with his hands trembling, Tim Caveny spread the calculated amount of powder along his iron trough, checked it to be sure it nestled properly under the orifices of his seven guns, then lit the right-hand end. With a powerful flash, the powder leaped from gun to gun, and as the first one exploded, Jake Turlock fired his monster.

From the point of view of massacring ducks, the timing had been exquisite, for the powder had ignited three of Tim's guns before Jake could fire his. This meant that at the first flash, hundreds of ducks had risen into the air, only to be knocked down by Jake's great gun, then punished by the last four guns in Tim's arsenal.

Never before had there been such carnage on the Chesapeake. In fact, the two dogs brought so many ducks to the skiffs that they showed signs of sinking; the watermen ferried dead birds to the ice shelf, stashed them and returned to fetch others. The dogs were exhausted.

Next morning, when the count was made, the partners had sixty-nine canvasbacks, thirty-two mallards, thirty blacks, twenty-nine teal and thirteen geese that they could ship to Baltimore. In addition, they had twenty-two pintails which they would sell for a few pennies each to the Negroes living in Frog's Neck, and a score of mergansers, which no one would eat because they fed on fish. Tim's imaginative arsenal, so dangerous to use, so lethal when used, had proved its merit, so the two watermen continued to fell trees by day and fire their cannon at night. Whatever money they obtained from Baltimore, they turned over to Paxmore.

As winter ended and the ducks flew north, Gerrit Paxmore finished building his first skipjack, and when it was launched he told the two watermen, 'This boat will sail better than any in the bay.' Turlock and Caveny were prepared to believe this, but they were taken aback when the Quaker added, 'I've kept thy money in our office. I'm prepared to hand it back, because thee doesn't have to take this boat . . . if thee doesn't wish.'

'Why wouldn't we?' Turlock asked angrily.

'Because,' Paxmore said quietly, 'I've done something with the centerboard.'

The three men went aboard and climbed down into the hold where they could inspect the bottom of the boat, and there Turlock and Caveny saw the damnedest thing their eyes had ever met. Instead of placing the centerboard in the middle of the keel—cutting a slim hole fourteen feet long right through the heart of the oak, then building around it what boatmen called the trunk to keep out the water—Paxmore had left the keel untouched, as the tradition of his family required, but had cut a hole parallel to it, thus offsetting the centerboard some eight inches to starboard.

'You goddamned fool!' Turlock shouted. 'This boat's off center. It'll never . . .'

'Friend,' Paxmore said gently, 'thee has no need to swear. Thy deposit is waiting.'

'But goddamnit, I asked you plain and simple about the centerboard. And you told me in your own words . . . Didn't he, Tim?'

'He sure as hell did. Why, this damned thing—it's a cripple.'

'Please, gentlemen. Speak less roughly. Thy money—'

'To hell with our money! We want our boat.'

'Thee is not obligated . . .'

It was dark in the bowels of the skipjack and the three men seemed like angry ghosts. The centerboard was sadly awry; indeed, to call it a center anything was ridiculous. The whole balance of the boat was destroyed, and Caveny could visualize it sailing crab-wise down the bay. Tears came into his eyes, and he showed Pax-more his hands, blistered for months. 'We chopped every god-damned timber in this boat. And what do we get?'

'A —— washtub,' Turlock said, using the foulest word he could conjure.

It was this ultimate obscenity that awakened Paxmore to the fact that he was in real trouble. He had assumed that by merely offering the men their money, he would be relieved of difficulties with his unusual craft; certainly he could peddle it to someone else, per-haps at a minor loss, and with the funds thus received, pay the two watermen for their work in felling trees.

'No!' Turlock said grimly. 'We want our boat and we want it now. You take that goddamned centerboard out of there and you put it in here, where it belongs.'

'That I will not do,' Paxmore said, and as he spoke his right hand fell protectively upon the unblemished keel, and only then did Tim Caveny realize that this unpleasant Quaker loved the new craft as much as he and Jake did.

'What we might do,' Tim suggested, 'is take her for a trial.' Turlock did not want to do this, lest he like the results, but Pax-more encouraged the idea. However, Tim had an additional idea: 'Suppose we do accept it, damaged though it is? How much reduc-tion in cost?'

'Not one penny,' Paxmore said. 'This is the finest boat on the bay, and if truth were told, thee should pay me an extra two hundred.'

'You are a son-of-a-bitch,' Turlock growled, and as he climbed out of the hold he said, 'I want to be let off this boat. I want nothin' to do with a goddamned washtub.'

'Let's give it a trial,' Tim pleaded, and he began to haul the mainsail, and every pulley, every rope worked so perfectly that he said, 'They're right. A sail like this does raise easier.'

They raised the jib, too, and then they swung the gigantic boom, two feet longer than the boat that supported it, and they could feel the power of the canvas overhead. There was a good breeze, and Caveny and Paxmore moved the skipjack into the middle of the Choptank—Turlock wouldn't touch sail or wheel—and she began to lay over to starboard, and the water broke white, and sea-gulls followed the new craft, and after a long while Turlock muscled his way aft and shoved Caveny away from the wheel.

Paxmore sat on the hatch covering, saying nothing. He could feel his boat responding to the waves and could visualize just how she accommodated to the wind. When Turlock called from the wheel, 'I think she needs more ballast forward,' Paxmore said, 'I think so, too.'

They christened her the *Jessie T*, after Jake's mother, and before she took her first trip oystering, the conventions governing skip-jacks were installed: 'No color of blue ever to board this boat. No red brick ever to be used as ballast. No walnuts to be eaten. No hatch cover ever to be placed on deck upside down.' And because of the extremely low railing and the massiveness of the boom, larger by far than that on any other type of vessel sailing the Chesapeake: 'Above all, when you work on deck, mind the boom!'

The *Jessie T* was worked by a crew of six: Captain Jake Turlock, in command of the craft and responsible for her safety; First Mate Tim Caveny, who took care of the money; three Turlocks, who manned the dredges in which the oysters were caught; and the most important member, the cook. From the day the boat was planned to the moment when the three Turlocks were hired, there had been only one candidate for cook: a remarkable black man renowned along the Choptank.

He was Big Jimbo, an unusually tall Negro, son of the slaves

Cudjo and Eden Cater. From his father he had learned to read and from his mother to carry himself with fierce pride. He was a gentle man, given to humor, and because of his rare ability with a ship's stove he knew that he was as good as the captain and better than the crew.

He resolved one possible difficulty the instant he came aboard. On a skipjack the three crewmen slept forward in cramped quarters. The captain, cook and mate—in that order—divided the three good bunks aft among themselves, and it had become traditional for the captain to choose the extra-long bunk to the starboard, the cook to take the next best one to port, with the mate getting the somewhat less convenient bunk across the back of the cabin; but on the *Jessie T* things worked out a little differently: one of the Turlocks who should have slept forward was a close cousin of Jake's and he announced that he would sleep aft, because he was sure the nigger wouldn't mind berthing in the smaller quarters.

So when Big Jimbo came aboard he found his bunk taken. Without even a second's hesitation, he politely lifted the gear out, placed it on deck and said, 'Cain't no man cook if'n he sleeps forward.'

He had made a mistake, and a serious one. The gear he had thrown out of the aft cabin was not the intruder's, but Tim Caveny's, the co-owner of the skipjack. When the Turlock lad had decided to move aft, Tim had seen a chance to promote himself into a better bunk, so he had preempted the cook's and had diverted Jake's cousin into the shorter aft bunk. When Tim saw his gear being thrown on deck, he started to raise hell, but Big Jimbo said softly, 'Mister Tim, if'n that's yours, I do apologize,' and he was more than polite in returning it to the cabin, where he placed it not in the bunk that Tim had chosen, but in the aft one.

'I sort of thought I'd sleep here,' the Irishman said tentatively, pointing to the cook's longer bunk.

'Cook sleeps here,' Big Jimbo said, and he used his words so sweetly that even the displaced owner was charmed. And then, before any ill feeling could develop, Jimbo assembled the crew on

deck and said, 'I brung me some milk and some cream, so we gonna have the world's best arster stew. You want she-stew or he-stew?'

'You cain't tell a she arster from a he,' one of the Turlocks said.

'I ain't talkin' about the arsters. I'se talkin' about the eaters.' He smiled benignly at the watermen and asked, 'What's it to be, she or he?'

'What's the difference,' one of the men asked.

'That ain't for you to ask.'

'We'll take he.'

'Best choice you ever made,' Jimbo said, and he disappeared down the hatch leading to his wood stove.

A she-stew was the traditional one served throughout the Chesapeake: eight oysters per man, boiled ever so slightly in their own liquor, then in milk and thickened with flour, flavored with a bit of celery, salt and pepper. It was a great opening course but somewhat feeble for workingmen.

A he-stew was something quite different, and Big Jimbo mumbled to himself as he prepared his version, 'First we takes a mess of bacon and fries it crisp.' As he did this he smelled the aroma and satisfied himself that Steed's had sold him the best. As it sizzled he chopped eight large onions and two hefty stalks of celery, holding them back till the bacon was done. Deftly he whisked the bacon out and put it aside, tossing the vegetables into the hot oil to sauté. Soon he withdrew them, too, placing them with the bacon. Then he tossed the forty-eight oysters into the pan, browning them just a little to implant a flavor, then quickly he poured in the liquor from the oysters and allowed them to cook until their gills wrinkled.

Other ship's cooks followed the recipe this far, but now Big Jimbo did the two things that made his he-stew unforgettable. From a precious package purchased from the McCormick Spice Company on the dock in Baltimore he produced first a canister of tapioca powder. 'Best thing ever invented for cooks' in his opinion. Taking a surprisingly small pinch of the whitish powder, he tossed it into the milk, which was about to simmer, and in a few minutes the moisture and the heat had expanded the finely ground tapioca powder into a very large translucent, gelatinous mass. When he was satisfied with the progress he poured the oysters into the milk, tossed in the vegetables, then crumbled the bacon between his fingers, throwing it on top.

The sturdy dish was almost ready, but not quite. From the McCormick package he brought out a packet of saffron, which he dusted over the stew, giving it a golden richness, augmented by the half-pound of butter he threw in at the last moment. This melted as he brought the concoction to the table, so that when the men dug in, they found before them one of the richest, tastiest stews a marine cook had ever devised.

'Do we eat this good every day?' Caveny asked, and Big Jimbo replied, 'You brings me the materials, I brings you the dishes.'

Dredging oysters was hard work, as events during the winter of 1892 proved. The season was divided into two halves, October to Christmas, when the oysters were plentiful, and January to the end of March, when they were more difficult to find. Since the *Jessie T* had an all-Patamoke crew, it returned to that port each Saturday night, bringing huge catches of oysters for sale to the local packing plants, and because those who sailed the skipjack were devoutly religious—even the profane Turlocks—they did not sneak out of port late on Sunday afternoon, as some did, but waited till Monday morning, an act of devotion for which they expected God to lead them to the better beds.

Captain Jake had enjoyed Christmas and was sleeping soundly this first Monday after the New Year, but at three o'clock in the morning his daughter Nancy shook him by the shoulder and whispered, 'Daddy! Time to sail.' He muttered a protest, then sat bolt upright. 'What time?' he asked, and she replied, clutching her nightgown about her throat, 'Three.'

He leaped from bed, climbed into five layers of protective clothing, then went into the next room, where he kissed his two other children as they slept. His wife was already in the kitchen brewing a pot of coffee and pouring out a quart of milk for him to take to the boat. She also had some strips of bacon and a handful of onions to be delivered to Big Jimbo for that day's stew.

Through the dark streets of Patamoke, Captain Jake headed for the wharf, and as he approached the swaying masts of the oyster fleet, he saw converging on the waterfront a score of men dressed like himself, each bringing some item of special food. They moved like shadows in the frosty air, grunting hellos as they met, and when Jake reached the *Jessie T* he was pleased to see that Big Jimbo was already aboard, with a fire well started.

'Brung you some milk,' he said, half throwing his parcel onto the swaying table. The cook grunted some acknowledgment, then reached for a bucket of choice oysters that had been set aside for this occasion. Placing a well-worn glove on his left hand, he began shucking the oysters, tossing the meat into one pan while pouring as much of the liquor as possible into another. 'Things look good,' Captain Jake said as he deposited his gear and went on deck.

Mate Caveny was prompt, and while he and the captain cleared the deck, the three Turlock crewmen came aboard, stowing their gear forward in the mean quarters. 'Cast off!' Jake called, and when his lines were clear and his two sails aloft, his skipjack began its slow, steady movement out to the center of the river, then westward toward the bay. Three hours later the sun would begin to rise, but for the present they would be in darkness.

It was very cold on deck. A brisk wind swept in from the bay, coming as usual out of the northwest, bitter cold from Canada. Captain Jake stayed at the wheel, standing before it and moving it with his left hand behind his back. The Turlocks patrolled the deck, while Caveny stayed below helping the cook.

Past Peace Cliff they went and into the channel north of Devon Island. Blackwalnut Point appeared in the dim light, while ahead lay the great bay, its waters ruffled by the heavy wind. It was cold, dark and wet as the tips of waves broke off to become whipping spray that cut the face.

But now Big Jimbo rang his bell, and all but the youngest Turlock moved below; he watched the wheel, standing in front of it, as the captain had done.

In the cramped cabin below, Big Jimbo had prepared one of his best he-stews, and when crackers were broken over the bottom of their bowls and the rich mixture poured in, the men's faces glowed. But as in most skipjacks, no one moved a spoon until the cook had taken his place at the small table and reached out his large black hands to grasp those of Captain Turlock and Mate Caveny, whose free hands sought those of the two crewmen. The circle thus having been completed, the five watermen bowed their heads while Captain Turlock uttered the Protestant grace:

'God is great. God is good.
And we thank Him for our food.
By His hand we all are fed.
Thank Thee, Lord, for daily bread.'

When he finished, all the men said 'Amen,' but they did not relax their hands, for it was now Tim Caveny's responsibility to intone the Catholic grace:

'Bless us, O Lord, for these Thy gifts which we are about to receive from Thy bounty, through Christ our Lord, Amen.'

Again the men said 'Amen,' but still they kept their hands together, for in addition to the two formal graces, it was the custom aboard the *Jessie T* for Caveny to add a personal prayer, and in his rich Irish accent he now asked God for special attention:

'We have observed Thy day with prayers and have sought Thy blessing upon our families. Now we ask that Thee guide this boat to where the arsters sleep awaiting our coming. Lord, make the harvest a rich one. St. Peter, guardian of fishermen, protect us. St. Patrick, who crossed the sea, watch over this boat. St. Andrew, who fished the Sea of Galilee, guide us to our catch.'

'Amen,' the watermen whispered, and spoons dipped into the golden-flecked stew.

They needed prayers, for their work was both hard and dangerous. When Captain Jake felt that the *Jessie T* was properly positioned over the invisible beds, he ordered Caveny and the three Turlocks to drop the two dredges, one port, one starboard, and when these iron-pronged collectors had bounced over the bottom long enough, he tested the wires holding them, calculating whether the load was adequate, and when he was satisfied, he ordered the dredges hauled aboard.

Now the muscle-work began. Port and starboard stood two

---

winches, powered by hand, and around the drum of each, the wire leading to its dredge was wound. Then the men, two to a winch, began turning the heavy iron handles, and as the drums revolved, the lines holding the submerged dredges were hauled aboard. Danger came when the iron prongs of the dredge caught in rock, reversing the handle and knocking out men's teeth or breaking their arms. Few watermen ever worked the oyster bars without suffering some damage from reversing handles; one of the younger Turlocks carried a broad scar across his forehead—'I like to died from bleedin'. Lessen I had a head like rock, I be dead.'

When the dredges finally climbed aboard, dripping with mud and weed, their cargo was dumped on deck, except when the load

was simply too dirty to work; then the men engaged in a maneuver that almost jerked their arms from their sockets. Alternately lowering the dredge into the sea a few feet, and yanking it back, they sloshed the great net up and down until the mud washed free. Only then were they allowed to bring it aboard with its load of oysters and shells.

Quickly the dredges were emptied onto the deck, then thrown back for another catch. As soon as they were back in the water, the watermen knelt on the deck to begin the sorting, and with deft hands well scarred by the sharp edges of oysters, they picked through the mass of dead shell and weed, isolating the living oysters which represented their catch. Their fingers seemed to dance through the debris, knowing instinctively whenever they touched a good oyster; with curious skill they retrieved each one, tossing it backward toward the unseen piles that mounted as the day's dredging progressed.

It was a custom aboard the skipjacks for each of the four men sorting the catch to throw his oysters into the corner of the boat behind him; this distributed the weight of the catch evenly across the deck of the boat, fore and aft, port and starboard. When the long day ended—dawn till dusk, six days a week—the *Jessie T* was usually piled high with oysters, yet riding evenly in the water because of the planned way they had been stowed.

Toward the end of each day Captain Jake, who did none of the sorting, began to look for a boat flying a bushel basket high from its mast. This was the buy-boat, and there was usually one in the vicinity. When it came alongside, the men aboard the *Jessie T* had to work double-fast. Into the iron measuring bucket dropped onto their deck by a boom from the buy-boat they shoveled their catch, and each time the iron bucket rose in the air and returned to the buy-boat, depositing the oysters into its hold, Tim Caveny at the railing would cry 'Tally one!' then 'Tally two!'—and so on until the fifth bucket, when he would shout 'Mark one!' Then he would begin again with 'Tally one!'

At dusk he would report to his crew, 'Twenty-two and three.' This meant twenty-two marks plus three tallies, or one hundred

95

and thirteen bushels. And each man would then calculate what that day's work had brought.

The *Jessie T* worked on shares. The skipjack itself received one third, divided evenly between the two owners, Jake and Tim, but they had to pay for the food, the cordage, the dredges. The captain received a third, which again he had to split with Caveny, who could just as easily have served as leader. And the four crewmen split the remaining third among them, except that Big Jimbo was recognized as such a superior cook that he received a little extra from everyone.

His position was anomalous. The four Turlocks hated Negroes and never hesitated in voicing their disgust. 'Goddamned spades killed my cousin Captain Matt—one of them gets out of line with me, he's dead.' They often made this threat in the presence of Big Jimbo, indicating they knew damned well he was descended from the murderer; but the cook himself was prized as a friend, as a most willing helper on deck and as the best galley-man in the fleet. 'When you sail *Jessie T*, man, you eat. Our nigger can outcook your nigger ever' time.'

The extraordinary contribution of Big Jimbo was demonstrated one gray February morning when the men were at breakfast, with the youngest Turlock at the wheel. The skipjack was heeling to starboard, so that the dishes on the crowded table were sliding, and Captain Jake called up through the cabin door, 'All okay up there?'

'All's fine!' the man at the wheel shouted back, but soon thereafter he cried in some alarm, 'Cap'm! Very dark clouds!' And then immediately, 'I need help!'

Captain Jake started for the ladder, but Ned Turlock, one of the three crewmen, beat him to it. With a hearty bound, the young man leaped up the four steps and made the deck just in time to be struck in the face by the flying boom, which had been swept across the deck by a change in the storm's direction. Ned was knocked into the turbulent water and was soon far aft of the skipjack without a lifebelt, but Captain Jake, taking command of the wheel, swung the boat about while everyone worked the sails in an effort to bring it under control.

As soon as the skipjack steadied and was on a course that might bring her near the thrashing waterman, who was struggling to stay alive, Big Jimbo tied a rope about his waist, then asked Tim Caveny to fashion a kind of harness, with smaller ropes lashing him about the shoulders and holding him to the main rope. When this was tested, the big cook checked to be sure that the loose end of the rope was secured to a mooring cleat, and then, without hesitation, plunged into the deep, icy waters. His arms thrashed wildly as he tried to stabilize himself, and one of the Turlocks cried, 'Hell, he cain't swim neither,' and Captain Jake growled, 'Niggers cain't never swim. Watch him with the hook.'

Big Jimbo, kicking his feet and flailing his arms, moved closer to the drowning man, but the force of the waves and the irresistible movement of the skipjack prevented him from making the rescue, and it seemed that Ned Turlock must drown. But on deck Captain Jake was willing to take great risks, so in the midst of the furious squall, he brought his boat around, almost capsizing it, and headed on a tack that would intercept his cousin in the water.

With a giant embrace, Big Jimbo caught the exhausted man, clutched him to his bosom and pressed water from his lungs as the men aboard the *Jessie T* pulled on the rope to drag the two men aboard. At supper that night, after the oysters had been sold and the profits calculated, the six watermen joined hands as Caveny poured out their thanks:

> 'Almighty God, Thou didst send the storm much like the one that swamped the fishermen on Galilee, and in Thy wisdom Thou didst sweep our sailor Ned from us. But just as Thou didst rescue Jonah after forty days and forty nights in the belly of the whale, so didst Thou urge our nigger Big Jimbo to dive into the rolling waters to save Ned. St. Patrick, patron saint of fishermen, we thank thee for thy intervention. Greater love hath no man.'

When the prayer ended, everyone had objections: 'The forty days and forty nights were Noah and the ark, not Jonah.'

'They were both a long time,' Caveny said. 'I thought Ned was gone.'

'Last week you said St. Peter was our patron saint.'

'A fisherman needs all the help he can get,' Caveny said.

'You should of finished the last bit.' And Captain Jake misquoted, ' "Greater love hath no man than this, that he lay down his life for his brother." '

'I didn't forget. I just thought Ned might take it unkindly, bein' told he was brother to a nigger.'

With the near-drowning of Ned Turlock, the suspicion that the *Jessie T* might be a bad-luck boat gained so much credence that Captain Jake found it difficult to enroll a crew. One cynic at the store reminded the men, 'Like I told you, that skipjack was doomed from the start. Its centerboard is out of whack. Side-assed, you might say.'

And one of the Turlock boys who sailed in it confided, 'Thing you really got to watch is Captain Jake. In the fall, when arsters is plentiful, he pays his crew a salary. Come winter, when they ain't so many arsters, he smiles at you like an angel and says, "Boys, better we work on shares this time." I ain't sailin' with him no more.'

When an Eastern Shore skipjack found itself unable to enroll a crew, it was traditional for the captain to make the big decision, which Captain Jake now did: 'Caveny, we sail to Baltimore.'

With only Ned and Big Jimbo to help, they headed across the bay, past Lazaretto Light, past Fort McHenry, where the star-spangled banner had flown that troubled night, and into one of the finest small anchorages in the world, Baltimore's inner harbor. Its merit was threefold: it lay right in the heart of the city; it was surrounded by hotels and stores and warehouses immediately at hand; and it was so protected by their tall buildings that no storm could imperil a ship docked there. Also, it was a joy for any ship's cook to enter this harbor, because on the waterfront stood the huge McCormick Spice Company, its odors permeating the area, its shelves crammed with condiments the cooks sought.

As the *Jessie T* approached her wharf in the corner formed by Light Street, where the white steamers docked, and Pratt Street, where the skipjacks tied up and the saloons clustered, Captain Jake warned his companions to be especially alert. 'We may have to pull out of here in a hurry,' he said. 'Jimbo, you guard the boat while Tim and me goes ashore to tend to our business.'

'Cap'm,' the big cook said, 'I watch the boat, but first I got to get me some spices,' and as soon as the *Jessie T* made fast, Big Jimbo was off to McCormick's, returning with a small, precious package which he stowed below.

Now Turlock and Caveny started toward the row of saloons, and as they swaggered ashore, Jimbo called out, 'Good luck, Cap'm. I be waitin'.'

There was one saloon, the Drunken Penguin, at which captains needing crew often had success, so it was natural that the two watermen should head there. 'What a fine sign!' Caveny exclaimed as he saw for the first time the besotted penguin leering at him. Turlock, ignoring the art criticism, banged into the swinging doors with his shoulder, and smashed his way into the darkened bar, standing for a moment to survey the familiar scene. When he moved to a table at the rear, two young men who recognized him as an Eastern Shore skipper quietly rose and slipped out a side door.

He and Caveny had a beer, then a plate of food from the free lunch. 'Many people droppin' by?' Jake asked the bartender.

'Nope,' the barman said, wiping a glass much longer than required. 'They's mostly at the other places.'

'They'll be comin' in,' Jake said as he attacked his food. 'Tim, fetch me another pickled egg.'

There was no action that first afternoon, and Caveny suggested they explore some other bars, but Jake refused. 'In other years I've found what I wanted here. We'll find it this time, too.'

Toward dusk laborers from sites nearby dropped in for their evening beer, and Caveny said, 'Reminds me of those great opening lines of Grey's *Energy:*

> 'Homeward at the close of day
> The weary workmen come.
> Tired with their honest toil
> And all lit up with rum.'

Midnight approached and nothing happened. 'I told you they was at the other bars,' the barman said.

'I heard you,' Jake grunted, and that night he and Tim slept sitting at their table. Dawn broke, and along Light Street came carriages with passengers for the early steamers, and soon Pratt Street was alive with draymen. The heavy business of Baltimore was under way.

At about nine o'clock in the morning the two watermen were wide awake, and Tim suggested, 'I ain't never seen Hotel Rennert. Let's see where our arsters goes.' So the two watermen walked a dozen blocks in the clean, brisk air, crossed a park and stood on the Belgian blocks that surfaced all the streets near the great hostelry. 'Magnificence brought down from heaven to earth,' Caveny said. When Turlock made no reply, the Irishman pointed to the towering façade and the beribboned doorman. 'It's an honor to provide arsters to such an establishment.' Again there was no response, so Tim plucked at his captain's sleeve. 'Jake, I think St. Peter, patron of us sailors, would look upon it kindly if we had a beer at the Rennert, seein' as how we help keep it in business.'

'St. Peter might look kindly, but that flunky wouldn't,' Jake said, pointing to his rough clothes and Tim's unshaven face.

'There's always welcome to an honest workman,' Caveny replied, and he strode up to the doorman and said, 'My good man, Captain Turlock and I provide the arsters used in your establishment. Would you extend the courtesy of allowin' us to enjoy a beer?' Before the surprised functionary could respond, Caveny said grandly, 'At our expense, of course.'

'Are you indeed oystermen?' the doorman asked.

'That we are,' Caveny replied, 'best of the bay. Which is why Rennert buys from us.'

'Gentlemen, the oyster bar is through that door. I feel sure you will be welcomed.'

Gingerly Jake Turlock entered the mahogany-lined room. There was the glistening bar of which he had heard, the black man shucking in the corner, the chalked board proclaiming the many varieties of oysters available, and three men in business suits having an early snack. It was a handsome room, ideal for the purpose to which it was dedicated.

'My good man,' Caveny said to the barman in charge, 'my mate and I catch the arsters you sell here.'

'Is that true?' the bartender said.

'As true as I stand before you like the honest fisherman I am.'

'And would you be wantin' to sample the oysters you've caught?'

'God forbid that we should come all the way to Baltimore to eat arsters. What we want is a cold beer.'

'And that you shall have,' the barman said. 'Compliments of the Rennert.'

'We can pay,' Caveny said.

'I'm sure you can, but we rarely see our oystermen, and this beer is on the house.'

Caveny sipped his beer as if he were a gentleman, making various observations on the quality of the hotel. As he placed his glass on the bar, depositing it gently with ten fingers embracing it, he asked, 'Would you be offended, sir, if we tipped rather more handsomely than is the custom?'

'From sailors like yourselves . . .'

'Watermen,' Caveny corrected, and onto the bar he tossed a sum of coins which would have covered not only the two beers but also a generous tip. 'This is a grand hotel,' he told Turlock as they returned to the street, but Jake merely said, 'Back to the Drunken Penguin. You never know when they'll straggle in.'

The first prospect arrived at two that afternoon, an Englishman about twenty-four years old, seedy, bleary-eyed, underfed. He had just enough money to purchase a beer, which entitled him to gorge on the free lunch.

Turlock, watching his ravenous appetite, nodded to Caveny, who moved to the bar. 'From the fair city of Dublin, I'm sure.'

'London,' the Englishman said.

'None finer in the world, I always say. Would you be offended if I suggested another beer?'

The young man was not disposed to argue about such an invitation, but when the drink was paid for, and the glass stood empty on the bar, he discovered the heavy cost of this courtesy, for suddenly he was grabbed from behind by the strong arms of a man he could not see, and his generous friend Timothy Caveny was bashing him in the face. He fainted, and when he revived, found himself bound hand and foot in the cabin of a strange boat, with a very large black man standing guard and threatening to knife him if he made one move.

Jake and Tim returned to the Drunken Penguin, resumed their seats at the back table and waited. After dark a young man came into the bar, loudly announced he was from Boston, waiting for his ship to arrive from New Orleans; he lounged awhile, had a desultory beer and picked at the spiced beets, licking his fingers as he finished. He was a sturdy young fellow, and Caveny doubted that he could be easily subdued, so as the Bostonian looked aimlessly about the bar, Tim approached the bartender to make a whispered offer. It was accepted, and when Tim took his place at the young man's elbow to propose a drink in honor of the great port of Boston, where Tim had served in many different ships, the glass was ready.

The Bostonian took one sip, looked at the bubbles, then placed the glass on the bar. 'Drink up!' Tim said brightly, gulping down a large portion of his own drink.

'I'd like a pickled beet,' the young sailor said.

'Best food in the world with beer,' Caveny said as he passed the glass bowl along.

The sailor ate two beets, took three gulps of his beer and fell flat on the floor. 'Grab his feet!' Captain Turlock ordered, and watchers at the bar, who had seen this operation before, stepped reverently back as Jake and Tim lugged their second hand to the *Jessie T*.

When a crew had been conscripted in this way, a captain was afraid to put into port over weekends lest his men desert. He stayed out on the Chesapeake during the whole fall season, loading oysters onto the buy-boats, picking up fresh food from them when necessary and watching his shanghaied men every minute to prevent their escape.

'Don't feel sorry for yourselves,' Captain Turlock told the two men. 'You get paid just like everyone else. By Christmas you'll be rich.'

The impressed seamen had to work like slaves. They threw the dredges into the water; they pulled them up; they sloshed them when there was mud; they stayed on their knees hours and days at a time picking through the haul; and when the buy-boat came, it was they who shoveled the oysters into the metal buckets.

Oystermen had a hundred clever tricks for hoodwinking shanghaied helpers: 'Well, you see, the earnin's I've been quotin' ain't clear profit. You've got to pay for the clothes we provide, the gloves, and so forth.' They also had to pay for their food. Also

deducted were fees for mending the dredges, the cost of new ropes.

Captain Turlock favored a simpler method: 'You men are gettin' richer by the day.'

'When can we go ashore?' the Englishman asked.

'You mean, when can you leave our boat?'

'In a manner of speaking, yes.'

'At Christmas,' Turlock promised, and Caveny added, 'On that holy day all men yearn to be with their families.'

During the third week of December, when ice formed on fingers, the two impressed seaman came to the aft cabin and demanded to speak with Turlock. 'We want your promise that we'll be off this boat by Christmas.'

'You have my solemn promise,' Turlock said. And then, to make the deal binding, he added, 'Mr. Caveny will swear to that, won't you, Tim?'

'As sure as the moon rises over Lake Killarney,' Caveny assured them, 'you'll be off this boat by Christmas.'

Two days before that holiday, when the last buy-boat had loaded itself with oysters, Captain Turlock convened his crew in the galley and said brightly, 'Jimbo, if one of the lads could fetch you some milk at Deal Island, could you make us a mess of he-stew?'

'I likes to,' the big cook said, and Turlock studied the two shanghaied crewmen. 'You go,' he said to the Bostonian. Then, as if changing his mind for some deep philosophical reason, he said to the smaller man, 'Better you take the pail. I want to talk wages with this one.' So the Englishman grabbed the pail and went on deck.

Caveny, Jimbo and Ned Turlock followed him up to maneuver the *Jessie T* into the dock at Deal Island, so that the Englishman could step ashore to find his milk. While this was under way, Captain Turlock engaged the Boston man in serious conversation. 'Where will you be headin' with the pay we're givin' you?'

'Home. I've a family waiting.'

'They'll be proud of the money you're bringin' 'em.' The young man smiled bitterly, and Turlock said reassuringly, 'You mustn't feel angry. This is the way of the sea. You've learned about arsters and you've saved some money.'

Such moralizing was repugnant, in view of Turlock's harsh commands on this cruise, and the Bostonian rose in some anger to go above, but the captain detained him by holding on to his arm. 'Sit down, young fellow. We've taken a lot of arsters this trip and you'll be takin' a lot of money to Boston.' He added other sanctimonious truisms, at the end of which the young man said, 'Captain Turlock, you're a fraud. You're an evil man, and you know it.' In disgust he moved toward the ladder, but this time Turlock interposed himself physically, saying, 'I cannot allow you to depart in bitterness . . . before we've discussed your wages.' And the talk continued.

On deck the others understood why their captain was keeping the Bostonian below, for when the Englishman started ashore with his pail, Caveny yelled, 'The house at the far end,' and as the young man started off toward the little fishing village, the Irishman gave a signal, and Ned Turlock at the wheel swung the skipjack away from the dock and back into the bay.

'Hey!' the young man shouted as he saw his boat, and his wages, pull away. 'Wait for me!'

There was no waiting. Relentlessly the oyster boat left the island and the young man standing with his empty pail. He was beached, 'paid off with sand,' as the watermen said of this common practice, and if he was lucky, he could straggle back to Baltimore at the end of two or three weeks, without recourse or any chance of ever recovering his wages for long months of work. Tim Caveny, watching him standing by the shore, said to his two companions, 'I told him he'd be ashore by Christmas.'

When the *Jessie T* was well out from the dock, so that the abandoned man could no longer be seen, Captain Turlock bellowed from below, 'Mr. Caveny, come down here and pay this man!'

When Caveny appeared in the galley, Turlock said forthrightly, 'This man has honest grievances, which he's expressed openly. Calculate every penny we owe him and pay him in full. I want him to remember us with kindness.' And he went on deck, where he took the wheel.

With all the Irish charm at his command, Caveny reached for his account books, spread them on the table and assured the Bostonian, 'You've worked hard and you've earned every penny,' but as he was about to start handing over the cash, there was a wild clatter on deck. Noises that could not be deciphered shattered the air and from them came Captain Turlock's agonized cry: 'On deck. All hands.'

The young sailor from Boston leaped automatically up the companionway, not noticing that the paymaster remained stolidly at the table. Bursting through the cabin door and leaping forward to help in whatever emergency had struck, he arrived on deck just in time to see the massive boom sweeping down on him at a speed that was incredible. With a great cry he thrust his hands before his face, failed to break the blow and screamed as the thundering boom pitched him wildly into the muddy waves.

Now the four Patamoke men lined the railing of their skipjack and shouted instructions: 'You can make it to shore. Just walk. Put your feet down and walk.'

They were distressed when he flopped and flailed, too terrified by his sudden immersion to control himself. 'Just walk ashore!' Captain Turlock bellowed. 'It's not deep!'

At last the young fellow understood what the men on the disappearing boat were trying to say. Stumbling and cursing, he gained his footing, found the water no deeper than his armpits and started the long, cold march to Deal Island.

'It's a Christmas he'll never forget,' Tim Caveny said as the sailor struggled to safety. There were now only four to share this season's riches, and when they gathered for their evening meal, two days before Christmas, they joined hands and listened attentively as Tim Caveny prayed:

'Merciful and all-seein' God who protects those who go upon the waves, we are poor fishermen who do the best we can. We

go forth in our little boat so that others can eat. We toil in blizzards so that others can bide at home. We thank Thee that Thou hast brought us safely through this long and dangerous cruise, and we ask Thy continued blessing on our wives and children.'

Oyster dredging had ended for 1892; this night the buy-boats would rest in Baltimore. Tenderly the *Jessie T* came about, steadied her sails and headed home. The watermen would always remember that Christmas as one of the best in their lives, for the weather was crisp, with a bright sun during the day and a helpful mistiness in the moonless nights. They had a lot of hunting to catch up with, because guarding their shanghaied crew had prevented them from enjoying their guns during the prime months of November and December; they went out every night.

It was during the sail back home one morning that Tim Caveny cleverly put his finger on the considerable danger they might run if Captain Jake proceeded with his plan for restaffing the *Jessie T*, now that the Englishman and the Bostonian had departed. Turlock had mentioned the problem to Big Jimbo, who said, 'You ain't got no trouble, Cap'm. I knows two men like to drudge.' But when the cook returned with the would-be crew, Tim saw that each was very big and very black.

Without bothering to take his partner aside, he asked, 'Jake, you think it smart to hire 'em both?'

'They look strong.'

'But it would make three white, three black. And you know how niggers like to plot against white folk.'

Jake studied the three black men, and although their faces were placid, he could easily visualize them launching a mutiny. Turning to Big Jimbo, he asked abruptly, 'Weren't it your daddy that murdered my grandfather's brother?'

'Maybe it was your grandfather stole my daddy as a slave,' the cook replied evenly.

'Tim's right,' Turlock snapped. 'We'll take one. Catch us another white man in Baltimore.'

So on the first day of dredging, the *Jessie T* was not on station. She was delivering a load of ducks to the Hotel Rennert in Baltimore, and after this was accomplished, Turlock and Caveny returned to the Drunken Penguin to inspect what the waterfront had to offer. They had not long to wait, for into the bar came a giant German wearing one of those gray sweaters with a double-folded neck and pants so thick they looked as though they could withstand a hurricane. He was obviously hungry, for he wolfed down three pickled eggs before the bartender could pour his beer, and while he was gulping a sandwich, Captain Turlock struck him on the head with a bottle. When he collapsed in the sawdust, Caveny ran into the street and whistled for Big Jimbo to come drag him out.

He was still unconscious when the *Jessie T* sailed, but when the skipjack cleared the Lazaretto, Jake summoned the Turlock boy from his position forward and said, 'Take the wheel. This one may be trouble when he wakens.'

With Tim's help he spread the unconscious German on the deck, then grabbed a belaying pin and advised Caveny to do the same. When they had secure positions from which they could defend themselves, Turlock called for the black sailor to throw a bucket of water over the German's face, but just as the young fellow was about to do so, Jake prudently called for Big Jimbo. 'Better stand here with us. This one could be mean.' So the cook joined the circle, and the water was thrown.

The fallen sailor shook his head and gradually awoke to the fact that he was aboard a moving ship. When he sat up, wiping the salty water from his face, he stared at the circle of faces, two white, two black. Assuming that Turlock was the captain of this craft, he asked in heavy accents. 'Where'm I going?'

'Arsterin',' Jake replied.

The German was obviously disposed to fight, but he saw the belaying pins and reconsidered. 'How long?' he asked.

'Three months. And when we pay you off, we bring you back to Baltimore.'

The German remained sitting, and after he had pressed the water out of his sweater he said, 'Otto Pflaum, Hamburg.'

'Glad to have you, Otto. Coffee's on.'

He was a splendid addition to the crew, a man of powerful energy and surprising dexterity in sorting what the dredges hauled up from the bottom. Knowing nothing of the bay's traditions, he did not think it unusual when the *Jessie T* remained on station, week after week; he enjoyed it when the buy-boats visited to pick up the catch, for this meant that for the next few days the food would be superior, and he had a ravenous appetite.

'You let him, he stay at table twenty-four hours each day,' Big Jimbo said admiringly.

'Only decent thing on this boat, the cook,' Pflaum said.

In the winter of 1893 the crew of the *Jessie T* came to appreciate how lucky they were to have found big Otto Pflaum, for once more they were confronted by their ancient enemy: boatmen from Virginia creeping in to encroach on Maryland waters, even though a compact between the two states clearly reserved those oyster beds for Eastern Shore watermen.

The Virginia men had three advantages: since their state was larger, they were more numerous; their boats were much bigger than the skipjacks; and for a curious reason no one could justify, they were allowed to use fueled engines while Marylanders were restricted to sail. Their swift, piratical craft could strip an oyster bank in an afternoon.

Naturally, the Choptank men tried to hold the invaders away, but the Virginians were able sailors and knew how to muscle the smaller skipjacks aside. They also carried rifles, and since they were not afraid to use them, gunfire was common; two Patamoke men had already been killed.

At first there had been no retaliation from the skipjacks, but the past year, after several blatant attacks, some of the Choptank boats had gone armed, and sporadic firing had broken out. In spite of the fact that Patamoke boats sailed under a constant threat of open warfare, Captain Turlock had been reluctant to arm the *Jessie T*.

'Our job is drudgin' arsters, not fightin' Virginians,' he told the men at the store.

'What you gonna do, they come at you with guns?'

'Stay clear.'

One of the captains said, 'Strange to hear you say that, Jake. Wasn't your kinfolk them as fought ever'body on the bay?'

'Yes, and we're mighty proud of what they done, pirates and British and all.'

'Then why don't you arm yourself?'

'Because a skipjack ain't no man-o'-war.'

So the *Jessie T* remained unarmed, and Jake's strategy worked, for he moved onto the beds early each Monday, and after prayers, hauled his dredges back on deck with huge catches. When the Virginia boats began to encroach, and he satisfied himself that they were armed, he withdrew, content to work the smaller beds inside the Choptank. But his retreat merely emboldened the invaders, and before long they were brazenly aprowl at the mouth of that river.

The Virginians were led by a daring boat whose arrogance was infuriating. It was a large bateau named the *Sinbad*, distinguishable for two features. For its figurehead it carried a large carved roc, the legendary bird with great talons; and the entire boat was painted blue, a color forbidden to skipjacks. The *Sinbad* was formidable.

This winter she challenged the *Jessie T*, almost running her down on a sweep across the beds. 'Stand clear, idiot!' the Virginia captain bellowed as he bore down.

'Run into him!' Ned Turlock shouted to his uncle, but the *Sinbad* was much too heavy for such tactics, and prudently the *Jessie T* retreated.

This encouraged the other Virginia dredgers; with impunity they paraded over the Maryland beds, scraping them clean with their powered boats. It was a sad experience for the Choptank men, made worse by the fact that Virginia buy-boats moved in arrogantly to collect the stolen oysters for sale in Norfolk.

Something had to be done. One evening four Patamoke skipjacks assembled at one of the beds to discuss strategies that might restrain the Virginians, and one captain who had a safe crew, in that none had been shanghaied, said that since he was going ashore, he would telegraph the governor of Maryland, requesting armed force to repulse the Virginian invaders. But when Pflaum heard the conversation he demanded loudly, 'They go ashore. Why we have to stay out?' and one of the captains, aware of Pflaum's status, quickly explained, 'Because your boat gets the biggest oysters.' Later the *Jessie T* crewmen laughed at the big German as he stood alone in the bow, trying to unravel this curious explanation.

The telegram achieved nothing, so the skipjacks that had put into Patamoke for the weekend acquired rifles, which they were prepared to use, and for two days Captain Jake was content to allow the other Patamoke skipjacks to patrol the Choptank while he sailed unarmed, but when the Virginians detected this strategy, they came right at the *Jessie T* and muscled her off the good beds.

Otto Pflaum had had enough. Storming into the cabin at dusk, he shouted, 'You, damned Turlock. You don't go into Patamoke, you afraid I jump ship. You don't buy us rifles, you afraid of *Sinbad*. By God, I no sitting duck, let them others fire at me, bang-bang. I want a gun!'

He got one. Next afternoon when the *Jessie T* tied up to a Baltimore buy-boat, Captain Jake asked if it had any extra guns for sale, and five were procured, so that on the following morning when the blue-hulled *Sinbad* bore down with her engine at top speed, it found Otto Pflaum standing forward and shooting at them with a repeating rifle.

'He hit them!' Ned Turlock shouted as the surprised Virginians scattered about the deck.

For the next few days oystering was pleasant, and as they sailed back and forth across the beds, Captain Jake had time to reflect on the excellent job the Paxmores had done with the *Jessie T:* She has her centerboard off to one side, but she sails better'n any boat on the bay. He remembered telling Caveny, 'No man in his right mind would build a boat with the mainmast so far forward, but it works. And do you know why? Because it's raked so far aft.' It was a curious mast: it not only rose from the innards of the boat at a severe angle, so that it appeared almost to be leaning backward, but its top bent forward, producing an arc which seemed certain to break it. The mast thus fought against itself, leaning backward but

curving forward, and it was this tension that made it so powerful; from it hung one of the largest sails ever used on a small boat, and because of the mast's design, the sail rode up and down with ease. It's a beautiful boat, Jake thought. Damned shame it can't just mind its business and drudge arsters.

But under the leadership of the enraged *Sinbad,* the Virginians had mounted a concerted effort to drive the Marylanders away from their own beds, and any skipjack that volunteered to challenge them received rough treatment. Gunfire became commonplace, and Captain Jake was always inclined to retreat, to protect his boat, but Otto Pflaum and young Ned Turlock would not allow the *Jessie T* to be taken off station.

It became a target for the *Sinbad.* 'Move back, you bastards!' the captain of that vessel would bellow as he brought his engine to full speed.

'Don't alter course!' Pflaum would shout back, and the *Jessie T* held fast as Pflaum and Ned Turlock stayed in the bow, blazing away at the invader.

Nothing was accomplished, but one night as the crew assembled for prayers, Ned Turlock said, 'Uncle Jake, when you got yourself this German, you got somethin' good.'

The camaraderie of the cabin was a strange affair, as Ned pointed out one night, 'Never thought I'd serve with two niggers, and both of 'em real good at arsterin'.' He was seated between the cook and the black sailor, eating from a common pot. 'Where'd you learn to sail?' he asked the younger man.

'Big Jimbo, he teached me.'

'He ain't got no boat.'

'He brung me to the *Jessie T.* When you was duck huntin'.'

'You ain't never been on water, prior?'

'Nope.'

'Danged, you learn fast. You watch, Jake, these goddamned niggers gonna take over the world.'

'You sailed, prior?' Caveny asked the German.

'Many ships,' Pflaum replied.

'You jump ship in Baltimore?'

'Want to see America.'

'This is the best part,' Ned broke in.

'And you're earnin' good money doin' it,' Captain Turlock said. All the men engaged in this conversation would later remember that whenever Jake stressed wages, Otto Pflaum listened intently, keeping his hands clasped over his belly, saying nothing.

'He was special attentive,' Ned Turlock would report at the store.

He was attentive, too, when the *Sinbad* swept back into action, for when the Virginia guns blazed, and a bullet struck Ned, knocking him perilously close to the railing, Pflaum stuck out a massive paw, dragging him to safety. Then, using his own gun and Ned's, he launched a fusillade at the Virginia boat.

'I think he got one of them!' Caveny cried, for in the heat of battle Otto performed heroically.

It therefore posed a grave moral problem when the time approached to throw him overboard. In whispered consultations Caveny said, 'We got to remember he saved Ned's life, more or less.'

'That's got nothin' to do with it,' Captain Turlock growled. 'Cruise is endin'. We got to get rid of him.'

Caveny brought Ned into the discussion, expecting him to vote for keeping Pflaum aboard and paying him honestly, but the young man was a true Turlock, and said, 'Overboard. We need his share.'

So it was agreed that during the first week in April, as the cruise ended, Ned would take the wheel, Caveny would keep the German in the cabin talking wages while Captain Turlock and Big Jimbo waited on deck with belaying pins in case anything went wrong when the boom swept Otto overboard.

It was a gray day, with the wind blowing, as it did so often, from the northwest. The bay threw muddy spray, and the dredges were stowed port and starboard, having crawled across the bottom for three unbroken months. Everyone was tired and even the buy-boats had retreated to their summer anchorages. The long voyage was over and the oystermen were heading home to divide their spoils.

Tim Caveny was in the cabin, his books spread on the table, explaining to Pflaum how the money would be divided. 'We had a good season, thanks much to you, Otto. We handle the money like this. One third to the boat, which is only proper. One third to the captain. One third to you and young Turlock and the two niggers, with ever'body throwin in somethin' extra for the cook.'

'That's fair. Best cook I ever sailed with.'

'I'm now going to pay you in full—'

'All hands!' Captain Turlock shouted as a tremendous clatter echoed on deck.

Later Caveny confessed, 'It could of been my fault. You see, I knew the call was comin', so I didn't react. In a flash Otto saw I had no intention of goin' on deck, even though there was supposed to be an emergency. So he give me a look I'll never forget, hitched up his pants, pushed his right hand into his belt and went slowly up the ladder. You know what happened when he reached the deck.'

What happened was that Otto knew the boom would swing in upon him; he was ready when it came, grabbed it with his left arm, swung far out over the bay as it swept past, and with his right hand produced a pistol, which he aimed at Captain Turlock's head.

'One of the most devious tricks I ever saw,' Turlock said later, for as the boom rode out to starboard, Otto Pflaum slowly made his way forward along it till he reached the mast. With great caution he lowered himself onto the deck, walking slowly aft toward the cabin. He kept his pistol aimed at Captain Turlock's head, and when he drew even with Jake he said, 'I stay in cabin. Alone. You take this boat to harbor. Quick.'

With calculated steps, feeling his way as he went, he backed to the cabin door, opened it, shouted down the hatchway, 'Caveny, you got two seconds to get out or I kill you!' He waited for the terrified Irishman to scramble onto the deck, then descended slowly into the cabin, locking it behind him.

For a day and a half the five men on deck went without food or water. They sailed the *Jessie T* as rapidly as possible back to Pata-moke, angry and cursing at the duplicity of this German who had pirated their boat, and when they docked at the wharf, and Caveny had been allowed back into the cabin to pay Pflaum his wages, the big German crawled up the ladder, pistol in hand, and made his

way slowly to the side of the skipjack. Without a farewell of any kind, he gingerly stepped backward off the boat, still pointing his gun at Turlock's head, and made his way to a waterside bar.

'How I catch a ship to Baltimore?' he asked the girl waiting tables.

'*Queen of Sheba*,' the girl explained. 'When she comes down from Denton.'

She was exceptionally pretty, a girl of nineteen who prided herself on her appearance. 'What's your name?' Pflaum asked, flushed with his share of the oystering wages.

'Nancy Turlock. My father owns that skipjack.'

'He's a fine man,' Pflaum said. And for two days he remained at the bar, waiting for the *Queen of Sheba*, telling extraordinary yarns to Captain Turlock's daughter.

The War

WHATEVER SLIGHT REPUTATION THE *Jessie T* MIGHT HAVE earned by her good oystering was destroyed when Otto Pflaum loud-mouthed it in the Patamoke bars that Captain Turlock had tried to drown him and that he, Pflaum, had been forced to capture the skipjack and hold it against five opponents for more than a day.

'Jake botched it,' the other watermen said, and again none would sail with him.

Normally, Turlock and Caveny would have gone to Baltimore to shanghai a crew, but they were afraid that Pflaum might be lurking there, so they swallowed their pride and permitted Big Jimbo to sign up another of his blacks. Thus the *Jessie T* became the first Patamoke boat to have three whites and three blacks; it was a cohesive crew, for Big Jimbo disciplined his recruits, warning them, 'You do right, they gonna be lots of black watermen. You mess around, no niggers never gonna see inside of a skipjack.'

But any pleasure Captain Jake might have found in his crew was dissipated when he brought the *Jessie T* into port one Saturday in late December to learn that his daughter Nancy had run away to Baltimore. 'I grew suspicious,' Mrs. Turlock said, 'when she started ironing her clothes. Then I noticed that whenever the *Queen of Sheba* came to the wharf she asked a lot of questions. So I kept a close watch on her, but last Tuesday she fooled me by ridin' up to Trappe and takin' the packet there. She's gone, Jake, and do you know who with?'

'Lew?' Jake asked. Turlock girls had a habit of running off with Turlock men.

'Would to God it was. It's that Otto Pflaum.'

'God A'mighty!' Jake cried, and he was all for sailing immediately to Baltimore to recover his girl, and Tim Caveny encouraged him, but they were prevented from leaving by shocking news that reached them. Two skipjack captains had sailed into Patamoke with the superstructures of their boats chopped up. 'We was drudgin' proper in our waters off'n Oxford when the Virginians swept in. *Sinbad* leadin'. They like to shot us clean outa the water.'

'You mean, they came into our river?'

'That's where they came.'

'Anybody hit?'

'Two of my crew in hospital.'

'What are we gonna do?' the embittered skippers asked.

'Do? We're gonna drive them right out of the Choptank.'

On Monday morning the *Jessie T* sailed out of Patamoke with a grim crew. All six men were armed, and Big Jimbo assured Captain Jake that his two black sailors were first-class squirrel hunters. If there was to be battle, the skipjack was ready.

But it was hardly prepared for what the Virginians did. Four of their power-driven boats lay off the point of Tilghman Island, and as the *Jessie T* moved down the Choptank, these adversaries, led by the *Sinbad,* moved in upon her, judging that if they could knock Jake Turlock out of the river, they would have little trouble with the rest of the fleet.

It was a most uneven fight. Captain Jake stayed at the wheel, while his five crewmen, including Big Jimbo, stationed themselves along the rail. The Patamoke men fought well, and some of their fire pestered the Virginians, but the invading boats were too swift, their gunfire too concentrated.

On one pass, bullets ripped into the stern of the *Jessie T,* and Captain Turlock would have been killed had he not dropped ignominiously to the deck. Infuriated, he bellowed for Ned to take the wheel, while he crouched behind one of the dredges to fire at the *Sinbad*.

At this moment one of the Virginia boats swept in from the port side and rained a blizzard of bullets at the skipjack. Jake, kneeling behind the dredge, saw one of Big Jimbo's men spin in the air, lose his rifle overboard and fall in a pool of blood.

'Christ A'mighty!' Jake cried, forgetting his own safety and rushing forward, but as he did so, sailors from the blue *Sinbad* fired at the wheel, thinking to gun down the captain. Instead they hit Ned Turlock, who stumbled to one knee, clutched at the wheel, sent the skipjack turning in a circle, and died.

It was a terrible defeat, and there was nothing Captain Jake could do to retaliate. He had to watch impotently as the Virginia Squadron raced on, seeking other skipjacks that might want to contest its presence. None did.

As the *Jessie T* started her mournful retreat to Patamoke, the four survivors gathered in the cabin for prayers, and Caveny thumbed through his Bible for that passage taught him by an old sailor with whom he had first served on the Chesapeake:

> ' "The fishers also shall mourn, and all they that cast angle
> into the brooks shall lament, and they that spread nets upon
> the waters shall languish."
> 'Almighty God, what have we done to deserve Thy wrath?
> What can we do to regain Thy love? Blessed St. Andrew,
> patron of fishermen, accept into thy care the souls of Ned and
> Nathan, good watermen of this river. Blessed St. Patrick, dry
> the tears of their women, and protect us.'

The *Jessie T* would have to find a new crew, and gloom was deep upon the Choptank as its watermen studied what they must do to repel the invasion from Virginia.

Jake Turlock was gray with rage. He showed the fury that had sustained his forebears in their dogged fights against pirates and British warships, for not only had he been forced to witness the murder of his two crewmen, but he had also seen the insolent Virginians invade his own river. He took a violent oath to be revenged, and with his whole being engrossed in trying to come up with a plan, he forgot his dog, paid no attention to the geese inhabiting his marsh and even allowed his long gun to go unattended.

But it was crafty little Tim Caveny who devised the tactic whereby they could punish the *Sinbad*, and it was so bizarre and daring that when Jake heard it, his jaw dropped. 'You think we could handle it?'

'Positive,' Tim said, his eyes dancing with joy as he visualized the surprise he had fashioned for the Virginians. 'But since they operate with four powerboats, we better find five or six Choptank crews willing to work with us.'

When Turlock approached the other skipjack men, he found them hungering for a final showdown. 'And that's what it's gonna be,' Jake assured them. 'They can have their engines. What me and Tim's got cooked up is better'n engines.'

But as New Year's Day approached, with the start of the winter dredging, Turlock had to face up to the fact that the *Jessie T* suffered from one deficiency. 'Tim, we got to have up front a man with no nerves.'

The two watermen fell silent as each reviewed the strategy, and finally Jake said hesitantly, 'What we really need—'

'Don't tell me,' Caveny broke in. 'Otto Pflaum.'

'The same. And damnit, I'm gonna swallow my pride and go fetch him.'

They crossed to Baltimore, going straight to the Drunken Penguin, where they elbowed their way in. Big Jimbo, of course, could not accompany them inside, but he did wait in the shadows nearby, in case things got out of hand. They were seated innocently at their customary rear table, drinking beer like two ordinary Eastern Shore watermen, when Otto Pflaum appeared. He still wore his extra-thick pants, his heavy sweater with the double roll at the neck, and he looked formidable. As soon as he saw the Choptank men he assumed that they had come to take his girl away, so he did the

prudent thing. Without taking his eyes off his enemies, he grabbed a bottle, smashed the end on a table, kept it pointed outward from his right hand, and advanced. Then, with his left hand, he broke the end off another bottle. Thus armed, he approached, whereupon Caveny asked in a voice of gentle Irish reasoning, 'Otto, dear friend, don't you trust us?'

The big German said nothing. He moved closer, placing himself in a position from which he could jab a jagged bottle into each face. Then he stopped, keeping the bottles close to the eyes of the men who had tried to kill him.

'Otto, sit down and talk with us,' Caveny pleaded.

'You want to hire me again?'

'Yes!' the Irishman said eagerly.

'Same wages as before? A swingin' boom?'

'Otto, you misunderstood . . .' Caveny was eager to explain that a failure in communication had been responsible, but the German pointed the broken bottle at him and growled, 'Shut up.'

'We need your help,' Turlock said.

'Doin' what?'

'Sit down. Put the bottles away.' Jake spoke with such authority that the big sailor obeyed. 'How's Nancy?' Turlock asked.

'She's pregnant.'

'You married yet?'

'Maybe later.'

'Otto, we need your help. You got to sail with us again.'

'Plenty sailors, why me?'

'The Virginians. They're drivin' us from the bay.'

Turlock had said the only words that could have excited this giant. Pflaum had seen the arrogant *Sinbad* and had fought against her, so he relished the prospect of renewed combat.

'This time, no boom?'

'There was none last time,' Caveny said gravely. 'A sudden wind.'

'This time, pay before I leave Baltimore.'

'Wait a minute!' Caveny exploded. To make such a demand was tantamount to an accusation against the integrity of the *Jessie T*, but Pflaum was adamant: 'We give the money to Nancy. But she gets it before we sail.'

This was agreed, and on the last day of the old year the *Jessie T* returned to Patamoke for the unusual fitting out that Jake and Tim had contrived.

When Otto Pflaum saw the magnitude of the big gun that Jake proposed for the bow he was staggered. 'That's a cannon!' Jake said nothing, merely pointed to the small cannonballs intended for the gun, and before Pflaum could comment, he showed him three more long guns, several kegs of black powder and larger kegs of lead pellets.

'What you tryin' to do, destroy the *Sinbad?*'

'Exactly,' Jake said grimly. He then invited Tim Caveny to show Otto the real surprise, for onto the skipjack the Irishman had lugged three of his deadly spray guns, each with a battery of seven barrels and a capacity of many pounds of shot. Otto was captivated by the ingenious manner in which Caveny intended igniting his guns, and cried, 'You must let me fire one,' and Caveny said, 'Our plan is for you to fire two.' But Jake interposed, 'No, we'd better save Otto for the two big guns forward.'

'Do I aim at the cabin?'

'At the water line. I'm gonna sink her.'

So Jake spent the first two days of January training his accomplices; practice rounds were fired far up Broad Creek so no one could spy, and when he was satisfied that his men could handle their arsenal, he headed for the Choptank.

The guns were kept under tarpaulin, so that the *Jessie T* looked like merely one more Maryland skipjack trying to earn an honest living. The plan was for two relatively unarmed boats from Patamoke to move in the van in a casual approach to the oyster beds that were in contention, and to allow the *Sinbad* to drive them away. Then, when the Virginia vessel came at the *Jessie T* to complete the sweep, it would be Jake's responsibility to bring his boat as close as possible to the enemy, keeping the blue *Sinbad* to port, for the guns were concentrated on that side.

This would be a risky maneuver, because the *Sinbad* sailors had proved they would not hesitate to gun down the opposition, but Captain Turlock had anticipated the most dangerous moment: 'You men at the guns stay low. It'll be hard to hit you. I'll stay at the wheel and take my chances.' He had improved the risk by building about the wheel an armored semicircle behind which he could crouch; his head would not be protected, but as he said, 'If they're good enough to hit me in the head from their shiftin' boat, they deserve to win.' It was a confident crew of eight—four white, four black—that entered the bay and headed south.

Two days passed without incident, except that the *Jessie T* caught so many oysters it was an embarrassment. 'We cain't side up to a buy-boat, or they'd see the guns and the extry two men. On the other hand, if we pile them arsters right, they'll form us a fort.' So the deck was rearranged to permit the gunners to hide behind their catch.

On the third day the ominous blue *Sinbad* entered the Choptank, prowled the edges of the Patamoke fleet, then made a direct run at the two lures set up by Captain Turlock. As expected, the Virginia boat drove the smaller skipjacks off, then came directly at the *Jessie T.* 'Thank God!' Turlock called to his men. 'We pass her to port.'

The hidden gunners kept low. Jake hunkered down behind his iron battlement, and the two boats closed.

The first fire came from the *Sinbad.* When its crew saw that the *Jessie T* was not going to back off, their captain cried, 'Give them another whiff.' Shots ricocheted about the deck, ending in piles of oysters. The fusillade accomplished nothing except to anger the Choptank men and make them more eager to discharge their battery.

'Not yet!' Jake called, and his men stood firm while the *Sinbad* grew careless and moved much closer than she should have. 'Wait! Wait!' Jake called again, kneeling behind his armor plating as bullets whined by him.

As he hid, he caught the eye of Otto Pflaum, finger on the great gun once owned by the master-hunter Greef Twombly. He saw with satisfaction that Pflaum was not only ready with this gun, but prepared to leap to its lethal brother propped against the bulwark.

'Now!' Jake shouted, and from the entire port side of the skipjack a blaze of powder exploded, sending a devastating rain of lead across the deck of the *Sinbad* and punishing her at the water line. Those Virginians who were not knocked down were so confounded that they could not regroup before Tim Caveny fired at them with another of his seven-gun monsters, while Otto Pflaum leaped to a second long gun and aimed it right at the gaping hole opened by his first.

The *Sinbad*, mortally wounded, started to roll on its port side and its crew began leaping into the water and shouting for help.

'Let 'em all drowned,' Turlock snapped, and with grand indifference the *Jessie T,* her centerboard side-assed, as her detractors charged, withdrew from the battle.

It was a triumphal return such as few naval centers have witnessed, for the victorious vessel came to the dock laden with oysters, and as Tim Caveny called out details of the battle, Otto Pflaum counted the iron buckets as buyers on dock hauled them ashore: 'Tally three! Tally four! Mark one!'

At the close he informed his fellow crewmen, 'Damn near record. Thirty-nine and three!' But the *Jessie T* had earned more that day than one hundred and ninety-eight bushels of oysters. It had won the right to say that the riches of the Choptank would be harvested in a responsible manner.

The victory of the Choptank men led to a series of events that no one could have imagined.

The fact that Captain Turlock was now able to berth each weekend at Patamoke allowed him and Caveny to go duck hunting, with such good results that the two watermen accumulated surplus income in the Steed bank.

Since Jake Turlock had grown sick and tired of hearing the men at the store downgrade his boat—he loathed especially their contemptuous description 'the side-assed skipjack'—he decided to get rid of her and buy the partnership a real boat with its centerboard where it ought to be. When he approached Gerrit Paxmore with

this proposal he found the Quaker willing to listen. 'I've been pondering this matter, Jacob, and have concluded that I've been obstinate in refusing to build in the new manner. There is a difference between an ocean-going schooner, whose keel must be kept inviolate, and a skipjack destined for bay use only, where the strain is not so great. I'd like a chance to build thee one to thy design.'

When the contract between Paxmore and the Turlock-Caveny partnership was drawn—'a first-class skipjack with centerboard trunk through the keel, $2,815'—Gerrit Paxmore asked the owners of the *Jessie T* what they intended doing with their present skipjack, and Turlock said, 'I suppose we'll find a buyer somewheres, even if she is side-assed,' and Paxmore replied, 'I think I can take it off thy hands,' and Caveny asked, 'You got a buyer?' and Paxmore said, 'I think so,' but he would not divulge who it was.

So the new skipjack was built, superior in every way to the *Jessie T*, and when it had been launched and given a couple of trial runs out into the bay, Jake and Tim concluded that they had bought themselves a masterpiece, and the former said with some relief, 'Now we can hire a white crew. You, me, three Turlocks and Big Jimbo in the galley.'

'Them niggers wasn't so bad,' Caveny recalled.

'Yes, but a white crew's better. Less likelihood of mutiny.'

'The niggers fought well.'

'Yes, but a white crew's better.' Jake paused, then added, ' 'Course, I'd not want to sail without Jimbo. Best cook this bay ever produced.'

But when he went to Frog's Neck to advise Jimbo that the new skipjack would be sailing on Monday, he found to his dismay that the big cook would not be assuming his old place.

'Why not?' Jake thundered.

'Because . . .' The tall black was too embarrassed to explain, and Turlock heckled him, charging cowardice because of the gunfight, a lack of loyalty to his crew mates, and ingratitude. Big Jimbo listened impassively, then said in a soft voice, 'Cap'm Jake, I'm takin' out my own skipjack.'

'You're what?'

'Mr. Paxmore done sold me the *Jessie T*.'

The information staggered the waterman, and he stepped back, shaking his head as if to discharge evil invaders. 'You buyin' my boat?'

'Yes, sir. From the day I could walk my daddy tol' me, "Git yourse'f a boat." He had his own ship . . . for a while . . . as you know.'

'What ship did Cudjo ever have?' Turlock asked in disgust, and Big Jimbo thought it best not to pursue the topic. What he did say was this: 'He tol' me, time and again, "When a man got his own boat, he free. His onliest prison the horizon." '

'Hell, Jimbo, you don't know enough to captain a skipjack.'

'I been watchin', Cap'm Jake. I been watchin' you, and you one o' the best.'

'You goddamn nigger!' Jake exploded, but the words denoted wonder rather than contempt. He burst into laughter, slapped his flank and said, 'All the time you was on deck, doin' extry work to help the men, you was watchin' ever'thing I was doin'. Damn, I knowed you niggers was always plottin'.' In the old camaraderie of the cabin, where these two men had worked together, and eaten and slept, Jake Turlock punched his cook in the back and wished him well.

'But you got to change her name,' Jake said.

Big Jimbo had anticipated him. When he and Captain Jake went to the Paxmore Boatyard to inspect the refitted *Jessie T* they found the old name painted out, and in its place a crisp new board with the simple letters *Eden*.

'Where you get that name?' Jake asked, admiring the condition of his old boat. 'That's a Bible name, ain't it?'

'My mother's name,' Jimbo said.

'That's nice,' Jake said. 'I named her after my mother. Now you niggers name her after yours. That's real nice.'

'She give me the money to buy it.'

'I thought she was dead.'

'Long ago. But she always collectin' money . . . fifty years. First she gonna buy her freedom, and the Steeds give it to her. Then she gonna buy Cudjo's freedom, and he earned it hisse'f. Then she gonna buy her brother's freedom, and Emancipation come along. So she give me the money and say, "Jimbo, some day you buy your-se'f a boat and be truly free." '

In October 1895 the skipjack *Eden* out of Patamoke made its first sortie on the oyster beds. It was known throughout the fleet as 'the side-assed skipjack with the nigger crew,' but it was in no way impeded, for Captain Jimbo had to be recognized as a first-class waterman. There was, of course, much banter when the other captains gathered at the store: '*Eden* like to went broke last summer. Cap'm Jimbo tooken her up the Choptank to fetch a load o' watermelons to the market in Baltimore, but when he got there the crew had et ever' goddamned melon.'

There was no laughter, however, when the black crew began to unload huge quantities of oysters into the buy-boats. And the bay might have been outraged in the fall of 1897, but not really surprised, when Randy Turlock, a distant nephew of Captain Jake's, showed up as a member of the *Eden*'s crew, which now consisted of five blacks and one white.

'Why would a decent, God-fearin' white man consent to serve with a nigger?' the men at the store raged at the young waterman.

'Because he knows how to find arsters,' young Turlock said, and in the 1899 season Big Jimbo's crew was four blacks and two whites, and thus it remained as the new century dawned.

In August 1906, when the two watermen were in their grizzled sixties, Caveny came running to the store with exciting news: 'Jake, I think we got us a contract to haul watermelons from Greef Twombly's place to Baltimore.' This was important, for oystermen spent their summer months scrounging for commissions that would keep their skipjacks busy; the shallow-drafted boats carried too little free-board to qualify them for entering the ocean, or they might have run lumber from the West Indies, as many schooners did. Also, the boom was so extended that in a good gale, when the starboard was underwater, the tip of the boom tended to cut into the waves, too, and that was disastrous.

So the watermen prayed for a cargo of farm produce to Baltimore and a load of fertilizer back, or coal to Norfolk, or pig iron from the blast furnaces north of Baltimore. Best of all was a load of watermelons from far up some river, for then, with a crew of three —Turlock, Caveny and a black cook—the skipjack could earn real money, passing back and forth across the oyster beds it had worked during the winter.

At the start of this unexpected bonanza Jake was in such a good mood that as the lines were about to be loosened, he impetuously called for his dog to come aboard, and when the Chesapeake leaped across the open water to scramble aboard, Caveny asked, 'What goes?' and Jake said, 'I got a hankerin' to take my dog along.' Before the sentence was finished, Caveny had leaped ashore and was bellowing, 'Nero! Come here!' And his voice was so penetrating that almost at once his Labrador dashed up, prepared for whatever adventure was afoot.

It was a pleasant cruise. The skipjack sailed slowly up to the far end of the Choptank to Old Man Twombly's farm, where they found Greef and the watermelons waiting. His first cry from the rickety wharf concerned the gun: 'How's the big one doin'?' And before he threw a line, Jake yelled back, 'We're gettin' about seventy-seven ducks a go,' and Greef replied with some contempt, 'You ain't usin' enough shot.'

While the loading took place, the skipjack's black cook caught himself a mess of crabs from the stern and fried up some crisp crab cakes. Greef brought down some cold beer and sat on deck with the watermen and their dogs, remembering old storms. Greef made the men a proposition: 'Five years ago I planted me a line of peach trees, just to see. They're producin' major-like, and I want to risk a hundred baskets stowed on deck. You sell 'em, you keep half the cash.' But when the peaches were aboard and the skipjack was ready for sailing, the old man took Jake aside and whispered, 'With that gun, you load her right, you tamp her right, you ought to catch ninety ducks on the average.'

The passage across the bay was aromatic with the smell of peaches, and when the cargo reached the Long Dock, the A-rabs

were waiting with their pushcarts, pleased to receive fresh melons but positively delighted with the unexpected peaches.

With their windfall profits, the two watermen trekked to the Rennert for a duck dinner, then visited Otto Pflaum and his wife, loaded up with fertilizer and sailed for home. As they quit the harbor they chanced to find themselves at the center of a triangle formed by three luxurious bay steamers, now lighted with electricity, and they admired the scintillating elegance of these fine vessels as they set out to penetrate the rivers which fed the bay.

'Look at 'em go!' Jake cried as the vessels went their individual ways, their orchestras sending soft music over the water.

'Classic ships,' Caveny said, and for most of an hour the Choptank men regarded the ships almost enviously.

The oystermen could not have imagined that these large ships would one day disappear entirely from this bay, as the Paxmore schooners had vanished and the Paxmore clippers. The classic ship that night was not the gaudy steamer but the quiet little skipjack, the boat conceived on the Chesapeake, tailored to its demands and adapted in every part to its conditions. It would endure after everything on the bay that night had gone to rust, for it was generic, born of the salt flats and heavy dredging, while the brightly lighted steamers were commercial innovations useful for the moment but bearing little relation to the timeless bay.

'They disappear mighty fast,' Caveny said as the lights merged with the waves.

Now the watermen were alone on the bay, and before long the low profile of the Eastern Shore began to rise in the moonlight, a unique configuration of marshland and wandering estuaries. 'We really have the land of pleasant livin',' Turlock mused as his skipjack drifted in the night airs, but when they approached Devon Island he fixed his gaze at the western end of the island, where a multitude of trees lay wallowing in the tide.

'I never noticed that before,' he said. 'That island's gonna wash clean away, one of these storms.'

The watermen inspected the erosion, and Caveny said, 'I read in a book that all our land on the Eastern Shore is alluvial . . .'

'What's that?' Turlock asked suspiciously.

'Land thrown here by the Susquehanna, when it was fifty times as big. You know what I think, Jake? I think long after we're dead there ain't gonna be no Eastern Shore. The land we know will wash into the ocean.'

'How soon?' Jake asked.

'Ten thousand years.'

Neither man spoke. They were sailing over oyster beds for which they had fought, beds whose icy catch had numbed their hands and cut their fingers, bringing blood to their frozen mittens. Beyond that spit, barely visible in the night, the *Laura Turner* had capsized, six men lost. Over there the *Wilmer Dodge* had foundered, six men gone. Around the next headland, where ducks rafted in winter, the *Jessie T* had driven off the invaders from Virginia.

Softly the skipjack entered the Choptank. Jake's Chesapeake still patrolled the bow, ready to repel invaders, but Caveny's Labrador lay prone on the deck, his head close to Tim's ankle, his dark eyes staring up at the Irishman with boundless love.

The Warden

THE RETURN OF GEESE TO THE EASTERN SHORE BROUGHT TWO men into confrontation. Amos Turlock believed that the huge birds had come back to him personally, and since his ancestors had hunted geese on the Choptank for more than three hundred years, he proposed to continue. Furthermore, he intended using the long gun which had blazed across these waters since 1827, and when the geese began to invade his marsh, as they had in his grandfather's day, he figured it was time to check on The Twombly, hidden like the infant Moses in rushes.

Hugo Pflaum, the game warden responsible for the Choptank, began receiving indications that his brother-in-law Amos might be on the prowl. One resident reported having heard a tremendous blast at midnight 'like the echo of Confederate cannon at Chancellorsville,' and another had seen mysterious lights toward two in the morning, moving slowly up and down the river. Backwoods families began having goose with greater regularity than their legal huntsmen could have provided, and there were telltale traces of fresh corn on fields which geese had picked clean two months before. Worst of all, whenever Amos appeared at the store, he was smiling.

The law prohibiting his behavior was explicit, and he was breaking it in seven respects: he was using a long gun absolutely outlawed since 1918; he was using a night light which blinded the geese, something no decent gunner had done in the past hundred years; he was shooting at night, strictly forbidden; he was baiting his marsh and the field back of his cabin with great quantities of ripened corn; he was hunting out of season; he had no license; and he was selling dead geese commercially. But he committed all these crimes with such innocent deception that Pflaum could never catch him.

'The average crook,' Hugo reported to his superiors in Annapolis, 'lurks furtively, leaves a blazing trail that anyone could follow, and makes a score of mistakes. I've captured all the great guns but Turlock's. I've arrested twenty-three farmers baiting their fields, and I doubt if there are three night-lights operating in the entire area. But this damned Amos Turlock, he does everything, every night, and I cannot catch him.'

'The stories coming out of Patamoke, Hugo, are damaging your reputation,' the regional manager said. 'You want extra men?'

'That I could use.'

So two extra wardens were dispatched to Patamoke, dressed flashily like ordinary dudes out of Philadelphia, and they approached Amos with an interesting proposition that he act as their guide for some goose hunting.

'It's out of season!' he snapped.

'We know that. But in Chestertown they assured us—'

'In Chestertown they don't know a goose from a duck.' He dismissed them, then ran to the store to warn his cronies. 'Two new wardens in town.'

'How'd you know?'

'They walked like wardens.'

So he laid low, and after two weeks the strangers returned to Baltimore, assuring the head office that they had thrown the fear of God into Amos Turlock. That night with one mighty blow The Twombly slew sixty-nine geese, and Turlocks eight miles upriver feasted.

The explosion of the gun was clearly heard in several homes facing Devon Island. 'Sounded like maybe an airplane busting apart in the sky. We ran out, but it was all dark. Then we saw this light in Broad Creek and my husband got his field glasses, but by then the light had vanished.'

When Hugo returned to his office in the basement of the court-house he studied his maps and concluded that Amos had shifted his operations away from his own creek and out into the spacious reaches of the major rivers. 'Well,' he muttered to himself, 'that means he's got to travel some distance with his cannon. That gives me a chance.'

Early one morning he slipped downriver in his powerboat to inspect the setting in which he would lay his traps, but on the return trip he spotted something which disturbed him almost as much as the reemergence of The Twombly. On the sloping field leading down from the Turlock cabin hundreds upon hundreds of wild geese were feeding, their fat bodies moving in the wintry sun, their long black necks extending now and then to watch for any trespassers. They had apparently been there a long time and gave every indication that they intended remaining; Amos had certainly baited this field with shelled corn.

Cautiously Hugo beached his boat, climbed ashore and moved toward the field. As he did, the goose sentinels spotted him, satisfied themselves that he had no gun, and quietly herded the flock to another part of the field. They maintained a distance of about forty yards; if the warden stopped, they stopped. If he moved, they gave him space, and this allowed him to inspect the field.

Not a grain of corn was visible; the geese were eating grass. If the field had been baited, it had been done with such exquisite timing that by two hours after sunrise every grain was gone.

But just as he was about to leave in disgust, Hugo decided to move to where the geese now clustered, eating furiously, and as before, when he made a motion toward that area, the stately geese retreated just far enough to keep out of range. Again he found no corn, but he did find something almost as interesting: on a bramble in the middle of the area in which the geese had been feeding most avidly he spied two heavy threads used in weaving canvas.

'Damn!' he growled, his thick neck jammed down into his collar

---

147

as he stared at the signals: At midnight he rolls a hunk of canvas out here, covers it with corn, attracts a thousand geese, then rolls it up before dawn and leaves no sign. Except these. Carefully he lifted the strands of cloth from the bramble and decided that each night for the next week he would inspect these fields for corn spread out on canvas, which left no telltale marks.

'Hey!' a harsh voice called as he placed the evidence in his wallet.

It was Amos Turlock, with two of his sons. 'What you doin' on my land?'

'Inspecting the clever way you bait your geese.'

'No baitin' here.'

'The canvas, Amos. That's an old trick and it'll put you in jail.'

'What jury . . .' He allowed the sentence to hang, and Pflaum backed off. What jury, indeed, would indict a Choptank Turlock on the evidence of two strands of canvas webbing? In fact, what jury of men from the store would indict him if he marched along the wharf with The Twombly and sixty dead geese? Half the jury would expect to get one of the geese when they delivered their verdict: 'Innocent.'

Hugo realized that since Turlock had been alerted, it would make no sense to try to catch him at the baiting game, but if the wily fellow could be tricked into using his gun, then Pflaum could confiscate it on sight without the necessity of a jury trial. So he allowed Amos to think that his focus was on canvas baiting; indeed, he came out two nights in a row to let the Turlocks know he was watching their fields, but what he was really watching was the cabin for some sign of where the family kept their long gun. He detected not a single clue.

On St. Patrick's Day, after drinking several beers with young Martin Caveny, and nodding to Hugo Pflaum as he prepared to drive his eighteen-year-old Ford back to the cabin, Amos Turlock took a long nap, from about seven in the evening till midnight. He then rose, looked for his son Ben and his Chesapeake Rusty and led them into the marsh. The dog had long since learned to make no sound as they approached the area where the gun was hidden, but when he saw it safely loaded into the skiff that Amos used, he leaped joyously for the sturdier skiff in which Ben would ride to pick up the dead geese. He was so intent on helping his masters on another hunt that he failed to notice the faint scent of a stranger, a man in a rowboat lurking off the end of the marsh.

The three craft moved silently out into the Choptank, drifted westward for some time, the two skiffs oblivious of the trailing boat, which kept at a safe distance. At about three in the morning, when the crescent moon had set, the skiffs rounded a point not far from Peace Cliff, where the Quaker boatbuilders lived, and there on the bosom of the river waited a raft of some thousand geese chatting quietly in the night. The skiffs separated, the one with the dog lagging behind to wait for the explosion.

The major skiff, the one with the gun, eased its way toward the raft, making more noise than old Jake Turlock would ever have made. Now the justification for this carelessness became evident: Amos Turlock flicked a switch and a huge headlight set in a triangular, mirrored box flashed on, illuminating the masses of geese and freezing them into position. The light came at them so suddenly and with such reflected force that they were powerless to move. Aiming the skiff right at the heart of the motionless geese, Amos took a deep breath, kept his body away from the recoil of his monstrous weapon and pulled the trigger.

Only when the two skiffs were loaded with the seventy-seven geese and Rusty was back aboard, did Hugo Pflaum reveal himself. He had them now. At night. Long gun. Light. Seventy-seven birds. Out of season. He could put these two in jail for life, but when he moved in to make the arrest he found Amos Turlock pointing a large shotgun right at his chest.

'Hugo, you ain't seen nothin'. You wasn't out here tonight.'

With considerable courage Pflaum pointed his flashlight at the gun he was so determined to capture. There it was, resting insolently in its chock, its heavy butt jammed into the burlap bag of pine needles, the ancient slayer of waterfowl, the perpetrator of outrage. But protecting it was his brother-in-law Amos with a shotgun and a snarling Chesapeake.

'Hugo, be a bright fellow and head home. Me and Ben won't

humiliate you. We won't say a word at the store.'

Pflaum took a deep breath and rested on his oars, keeping his flashlight focused on The Twombly. He was almost close enough to touch it. Damnation, he did want to drag that gun into custody, to be photographed with it, to terminate its scandalous life on this river. But he heard Amos Turlock's soft, persuasive voice: 'Make believe you never seen it, Hugo. Go on home.'

With a regret that would burn for the rest of his life, the game warden dimmed his flashlight, cranked his outboard and started the noisy trip back to Patamoke.

Ice

DECEMBER 1976 WAS FEARFULLY COLD, AND EVEN MEN IN their eighties could recall no similar season when every expanse of water, from the merest creek to the great bay itself, froze solid. Winds howled down out of Canada with such heavy burdens of freezing air that thermometers dropped to historic lows, and the weather station at the mouth of the Choptank announced that this was the coldest winter ever recorded. Not even the remembered freezes of the 1670s surpassed this brutal year.

It was a trying time for the Steeds; Owen had promised his wife respite from the thundering winters of Oklahoma—'You'll find the Eastern Shore a gentle place . . . a little frost now and then.' This became their theme during the protracted freeze. Mrs. Steed would rise, see the unbroken snow, the creeks frozen so solid that trucks could cross them, and she would say, 'A little frost now and then.'

The long weeks of subfreezing weather—the whole month of January with the thermometer rarely above thirty-two—did not inconvenience the Steeds insofar as their own comfort was concerned. Their new home was snug; the fireplaces worked; the Turlock boy who cut wood from the forest kept a comforting stack beside the door; and it was rather fun to test oneself against the bitter cold. They walked together, bundled in ski suits, to all corners of their estate, and found delight in picking their way across frozen streams or pushing through marsh grass that crackled when they touched it. It was a challenging winter but one warm in associations, and they discovered that what they had hoped for back in Oklahoma was happening: they were growing closer to each other. They talked more; they watched television less; and certainly they spent more time together both indoors and out.

The difficult part of the winter came with the birds. One morning Ethel Steed rose to look out her window at the familiar scene of snow and ice and saw to her horror that a whole congregation of ducks had gathered on the left fork of the creek, trying futilely to break the ice so that they could feed.

'Owen! Look at this!' He joined her and saw that these creatures were famished. For six weeks they had been cut off from grasses at the bottom of creeks and rivers; they had been able to dive for nothing; their feeding places were frozen solid.

The Steeds put in urgent phone calls to their neighbors, and the advice they got was concise and harsh: 'Mr. Steed, thousands of birds are perishing. Worst place of all is the creeks around your home. What to do? Feed them, damnit. Buy all the corn you can afford and scatter it along the edges of the ice.'

Without waiting for breakfast, they jumped into their station wagon, maneuvered it carefully down frozen roads and hurried out into the country east of Patamoke. They stopped at a dozen differen farms, begging for corn, and when they had purchased a load which tested the springs of their Buick, they directed other farmers to the Refuge, buying from them as much corn as they could deliver.

They hurried home with their cargo, broke open the bags and began scattering the corn broadcast along the ice, and before they were half through with their work, great flocks of ducks and geese moved in, sometimes to within six feet of where they worked, and it was clear that the birds were starving.

For three days the Steeds bought corn, spending more than a thousand dollars, but when they saw how desperately the fowl needed it, how hungrily they waited for the Steeds to appear, they felt more than rewarded. Never before had they seen waterfowl at

such close quarters, and when a flock of seventeen white swans flew in, emaciated and near death, Mrs. Steed broke into tears.

Her husband halted this in a hurry. 'Let's get the axes and break a hole in the ice. Those birds are dying for water.'

So in their fashionable hunting togs they worked until heavy sweat poured from their bodies, trying to hack an open space in ice two feet thick, and then Owen had an idea: 'I remember a Currier and Ives print in which they sawed the ice.' He fetched a long saw, and after making a hole in the ice, widened it out to an opening about ten feet on the side. Before he was done, more than three hundred birds had flown in to compete for the water.

For two days the Steeds did little but stay at the hole, watching the splendid birds as they ate and bathed. 'They'll explode!' Ethel Steed said, but the birds continued to gorge themselves. Then she began trying to identify them; with the aid of color plates she was able to spot the green-headed mallard and the copper-headed canvasbacks, but that was about all. There were at least twelve other breeds which her husband could rattle off: 'Black, gadwall, red-head, teal, scaup . . .' Once he had hunted ducks with a powerful gun and good eye; now he was content to feed them.

It was while endeavoring to explain the difference between a bufflehead and a baldpate that he had his bright idea. Running to the house, he telephoned Annapolis and after some delay got Admiral Stainback. 'Spunky, this is Owen Steed. Tulsa. Yes, good to hear you, too. Spunky, can you hire me a helicopter? I know you can't get hold of a Navy one. But there must be . . .'

The admiral, a crisp Oklahoma man who had done much business with Steed's company, wanted to know why his old friend should need a helicopter, and when Owen explained that it was a mission of mercy, saving a hundred thousand geese, he said, 'Hell, that would justify one of our choppers!' And he asked for specific landing instructions.

Within an hour a Navy helicopter landed at the Refuge, within fifteen feet of the barn, and was loaded with bags of corn. Admiral Stainback sat in back with Ethel, while Owen rode co-pilot to do the navigating. With graceful ease the chopper lifted into the air, tilted to starboard and swept at low altitude up one river after another, while the passengers in back ripped open bags of corn, scattering the golden kernels across the frozen rivers.

It was a trip that dazzled the Steeds: each pond of water, no matter how small, reflected from its icy surface the shimmering rays of the sun; each cove was a frozen diadem. Marvelously attractive were the thin strands of rivulets which in summer would go undetected; in frozen splendor they shone like veins of silver. The relationship of water to land was sharply defined; the mystery of the Eastern Shore lay revealed, this wedding of snow-covered land and bejeweled rivers.

Even when the bags were empty and their muscles tired, the Steeds did not want the flight to end, for they were seeing a wilderness of beauty that might never be repeated. Generations could pass before the shore would again be frozen as it was this day, so when Admiral Stainback asked on the intercom, 'Shall we head back now?' Owen said into his microphone, 'I'd like to see how the Choptank develops,' and Stainback said, 'Said and done. Pilot, fly to the headwaters.'

With lovely, falling, sideways motion the helicopter dipped low toward the mouth of the frozen river, then turned east and flew slowly up the river that Steeds had occupied for so long. There was the mansion, half eaten away by summer storms, its widow's walk collapsed. There was Peace Cliff and the red roofs of Sunset Acres, where the marsh had been. Here were the gaping, rusted girders of what had been the Paxmore Boatyard, and beyond it the new red-brick homes in Frog's Neck, replacing the burned-out wooden shacks. But it was east of Patamoke that the Choptank became most memorable, for here vast marshes spread along the shore, marked now and then by rotting piers to which the ancient steamboats had come, all white and silver and shot with romance; now the pilings were eaten to the water line and silt filled the harbors where women in bombazine had once waited for their lovers returning from Baltimore. How noisy it had been then; how silent now.

There were the long stretches of river totally unoccupied, looking much as they had in 1700, and up toward the end the vast, rust-

ing sheds at Denton where huge riverboats had once brought their cargos of guano from Peru. Beyond lay the flat fields of Delaware in which the river rose, and beyond them the vast Atlantic Ocean, whose waters salted the Chesapeake and all its estuaries.

As they flew at a few hundred feet above this frozen wonderland, Ethel saw from time to time some hole broken in the ice by mysterious forces; often the opening was no larger than a tennis court, but about it clustered thousands of birds, desperate for water, and often, at a distance from the opening, lay swans and geese and ducks whose feet had frozen to the ice, holding them prisoner till they died.

'We can go home now,' Owen said from his front seat, and like a homing pigeon the helicopter twirled, found its heading and crossed frozen fields to the Refuge.

There was one aspect of that fearful winter to which the Steeds would never refer; it was too painful.

One morning as Owen was shaving he heard the mournful cry

of the heron—'*Kraannk, kraannk!*'—and he looked out to see two gaunt birds, whose habits he had studied with loving attention, land on the ice and walk in long awkward steps to those spots at which they had so often fed, hoping to find them free of ice, that they might fish.

Desperately they pecked at the unyielding surface. Then, with mounting terror, for they were starving, they hammered at the ice with their feet, a kind of death-dance. Accomplishing nothing, they pecked again, their long necks driving sharp bills with a force which would have broken normal ice. But this was different, and the poor birds moved from spot to spot, frustrated.

'Darling!' Steed called to Ethel in the bedroom. 'We've got to do something for the herons.'

'Are they back?'

'They were. Trying to find open water.'

'Why don't they eat the corn? Or go where the ducks are?'

The water at the big opening was too deep for them to fish; corn was a food they did not eat. What they required was some wading place in which they could feed in their accustomed manner, and across the entire Eastern Shore there were no such places.

The Steeds would make one. All morning they sweated at the onerous job of breaking ice along the shore, and by noon they had laid open a considerable waterway. They were eating a late lunch when they heard the familiar and now-loved cry, and they ran to the window to watch their friends feed.

But in those few minutes ice had formed again and the birds found nothing. In panic they tested all their feeding places, and all were barren.

'What will they do?' Mrs. Steed cried, tears in her eyes.

Owen, studying the birds with his glasses, saw how emaciated they were, but had not the courage to inform his wife of their certain doom. The herons, stepping along like ballerinas grown old, tried one last time to penetrate the ice, looked down in bewilderment and flew off to their frozen roosts. They were seen no more.

The Race

IN EARLY MARCH OF 1977, THE ROWDY SKIPJACK CAPTAINS FROM
Deal Island rolled into town with a proclamation that struck at
the honor of the Choptank; blacks and whites rallied to defend
their river, and old animosities were forgotten.

What the Deal Island men said was that they were the champions
of the Eastern Shore and ready to prove it in a grand challenge race.
To insult the Patamokes they added, 'Since you need every advantage to keep up with us, we'll hold the race in your backyard, Choptank River, first week in October.'

The Patamokes pledged themselves to enter seven skipjacks, five
with white captains, two with black, but with the crews mixed
three and three. The old craft were cleaned up and sailors began
practicing the maneuvers required for victory, but the people or-
ganizing the race were unhappy over one deficiency.

'It would look better . . . by that we mean that the papers and
television . . . Hell, you got to have the *Eden* in there. Oldest sur-
viving skipjack, and all that.'

The Patamoke captains agreed that it would be a fine idea to
have the side-assed skipjack participate in the race, but she had not
sailed for some years and it was generally assumed that her days
were done. When the experts went out to survey her, tied up be-

hind the ruins of the Paxmore Boatyard, they confessed that she was not much.

But when Owen Steed heard of the problem, he said abruptly, 'I'll provide the funds to restore her. That is, if you can get Pusey Paxmore to supervise repairs.' The committee hastened to Peace Cliff, where Pusey told them firmly that he was too old and no longer knew enough, but he did direct them to a nephew who had once built a skipjack, and this Paxmore joined the effort.

When the refurbished boat stood on blocks beside the harbor, her mast raked and glistening in new spar finish, the question arose as to her crew. She was the property of the Cater family; a stoop-shouldered man named Absalom held title and he owned a fine reputation at oystering, bold in defending his location against competition.

But when Steed and the committee went to Absalom they found him a testy man. 'Ain't takin' her out.'

'But Captain Boggs at Deal Island . . .'

'To hell with him.' Absalom Cater was the rugged new-type black who would tolerate no affront to his personal dignity.

'Mr. Cater, we'd really like to have you—'

'Name's Absalom.'

'Goddamnit!' Steed snapped in oil-field anger. 'I spent thirty years in Oklahoma disciplining myself to call you sons-of-bitches Mister. Now you snarl at me for doing so. What do you want to be called? Negro, black, colored—you name it.'

Absalom laughed. 'My problem is to discipline myself to stop callin' you white-asses Mister. Now what in hell do you want, Steed?'

'I want you to assemble a crew that will win this race. We're providing you with a damned good boat.'

'There's a boy shucks arsters at Tilghman Island. He knows how to sail with me. And Curtis from Honga. That's three blacks. You pick three whites.'

This was an insolent challenge, and it excited the imagination of the white watermen. 'Turlocks used to own the *Eden,* so we'll ask Amos.'

'He's almost seventy.'

'He can cook. And in a fight he's very mean.'

'Cavenys always worked this skipjack, so we'll invite Martin. And the Pflaum family. Hugo's stupendous in water.'

It was a menacing crew that assembled to give the *Eden* her trials, and a Baltimore reporter wrote: 'They resemble pirates about to loot a burning plantation.' Lanky Amos Turlock had only a few teeth; Martin Caveny, round and sly, looked like some henchman guarding a castle keep; and Hugo Pflaum, past seventy, still had the thick, squashed neck of his Rhineland ancestors. The three blacks at least looked like sailors: Captain Absalom big and dangerous, his two helpers lean and ready for a brawl.

With such a crew the *Eden* caught the fancy of newspaper and television people; incidents in her history were resurrected: built in 1891; captained by that Jake Turlock who defeated the Virginians in the Battle of the Bay; captured single-handed by Otto Pflaum from five armed watermen; the boat of Big Jimbo Cater, first and best of the black captains. 'Besides which,' wrote the proud reporter from the *Bugle,* 'she is the only side-assed skipjack in history, but she is given slight chance in the race because she cannot perform well on the starboard tack.'

The reporter had it backward. Every ship, every boat that moves under sail goes better on one tack than the other. Some mysterious combination of forces resulting from the interrelationship of mast, boom, keel and curvature makes one boat perform best on the starboard tack while another of almost identical design excels on the port. Like twins who share identities but who develop differentiated skills, the skipjacks varied, and Captain Absalom knew that his advantage lay when the wind blew from the starboard side, for then the offset centerboard cooperated with the tilted keel to produce maximum speed.

'I think we got her tuned just right,' he assured Mr. Steed.

Once when the black-white crew was practicing on the Chesapeake, Amos Turlock, coming up from the galley, spotted a chance to pick up some easy money. An expensive yacht had gone aground on the unmarked mud flats that rested just under the surface of the water where the western end of Devon Island had once stood. It was a perilous spot, which had not yet been properly buoyed, and the yacht's crew could be forgiven for going aground there.

'Halloo!' Turlock shouted. 'You need help?'

'We need a tow,' came the cry.

'We haven't the power to get you off'n there.'

'Could you get us a tugboat? We've radioed the Coast Guard, but they have nothing.'

'I can get you off,' Turlock called as the *Eden* closed.

'Watch out!' the yacht captain cried. 'You'll ground.'

'We draw two feet, centerboard up.'

'That's a hell of an advantage.'

'In these waters, yes. Mister, I can get you off without scarrin' the paint. Fifty dollars.'

'Jump to it.'

'It's a deal?' Turlock asked suspiciously. When the yachtsman assented, Amos yelled, 'Caveny, break out the lines. You know what to do.'

The yacht had gone aground because its construction required a massive keel reaching eight feet below water line, and it was this bulbous steel projection which had imbedded itself in mud. No possible tow from the *Eden* would break this loose, and the people on the yacht could not imagine what the motley crew on the skipjack had in mind.

It was simple. Caveny climbed into the *Eden's* rowboat, brought one end of a long rope with him, pulled himself onto the deck of the yacht, where he immediately clawed his way as high up the mast as he could go. There he fastened the rope securely to the spreader and signaled to Turlock back on the *Eden* that all was ready.

Slowly the skipjack moved away from the yacht, and as it did so, the line tightened, but there was no possibility that the frail craft could break the heavy yacht free, and the grounded sailors shouted, 'Careful! You'll part the line!'

It was never Turlock's intention to exert much pulling power; what he wanted to do was maintain pressure until the line high on the mast pulled the yacht over on its port side. 'Watch out, stupid!' one of the yachtsmen shouted as the boat began to list. 'You'll cap-size us!'

But Turlock maintained his gentle pulling, and slowly the yacht came down until its mast was almost parallel to the water; then the miracle on which he relied began to eventuate. What had been a massive yacht with an eight-foot keel was being converted into a bizarre craft with less than three inches of wood below the water line, and the huge bulbous keel stuck at an angle in the mud. The buoyancy of the new boat was so great that it began to suck the keel loose.

'Keep that line fast!' Turlock called, and everyone watched as the mast came down to touch the water, but as soon as it did, the yacht broke free, and with only a modest wind in her sails, the skip-jack was able to pull the heavier craft out into deep water. Quickly she righted herself, and the yachtmen cheered.

When it came time for the captain to hand over the fifty dollars, one of his crew complained, 'A lot of money for six minutes' work,' and Turlock said, 'Five dollars for doin', forty-five for knowin'.'

The pre-race meeting of skipjack crews was held at the Patamoke Club, and the mood was established by Captain Boggs, a towering black from Deal Island, known to his men as the Black Bastard: 'The *Nelly Benson* observes on'y one rule. "Stand back, you sons-of-bitches."'

Another Deal Islander said, 'This here is a race of workin' boats. Each skipjack to carry two dredges, a pushboat aft on davits, two anchors and full gear.'

One of the Patamoke men suggested a triangular course, but the Deal Islanders protested, 'We're racin' in your water. We state the rules. If the southerly wind holds, a run up the river, turn and beat back.'

That was it, a clean-cut rugged race of up-and-back with no furbelows or fancy diagrams. When this was agreed, the drinking began and some of the crews did not get to bed till dawn. Owen Steed, who by now was totally immersed in the race, got his men

home reasonably early and felt that the *Eden* had a good chance, unless Captain Boggs got an early edge, in which case he would be tough to beat.

Prizes for the race were not exorbitant: $75 to every boat that lined up for the start, and an additional $50 to each one that finished. The *Bugle* awarded a silver cup plus first prize of $100, second of $50 and third of $25, but most of the crews put together purses for wagers against boats of their class. The Deal Island men were especially eager to gamble, and Captain Boggs' *Nelly Benson* would go to the line with some $400 placed against various other boats.

The commodore for the race was a surprise, and a pleasant one. By acclamation, the watermen wanted Pusey Paxmore to serve as starter; in the old days he had been a man aloof, working at the White House and rather withdrawn from river life, but now that he had served time in jail he was more like them, and they insisted that since his family had built the oldest boats in the competition, the *Eden* and two others, his presence was obligatory. He had wanted to decline, but the Steeds would not permit it.

Since the race occurred in October, just before the start of the oystering season, the twenty-three skipjacks were in prime condition: all had been hauled out to have their bottoms painted, and all had been cleaned up on deck, their dredges neatly stacked, their lines coiled. Mr. Steed had purchased a complete new dress for the *Eden:* for halyards dacron rigging because of its inflexible strength; for docking lines and anchor cable nylon because it did yield. He had gone to Henry Brown down at the tip of Deal Island for new sails and he had specified canvas rather than dacron because the stitching in the latter chafed too easily. In its eighty-six years the *Eden* had rarely looked better.

The race was to start at the edge of the mud flats west of Devon Island, run up to Patamoke Light, turn it and tack back to a line between Devon and the mainland. A skipjack race started in a peculiar way: the boats jockeyed till they were in a straight line, then dropped anchors and lowered sails, waiting for the gun that would spring them loose.

It was a tense moment, for the honor of every settlement on the shore was at stake—the rough watermen of Deal Island against the dudes of the Choptank. Each boat had a crew of six experts, plus seven or eight casual hands to man the lines. The *Eden* had five extra Turlocks and two Caters, each with his own job to do. Little Sam Cater, aged nine, would perch as far aft as posible and stare at the water, prepared to utter his warning cry, 'Mud! Mud!'

'You can fire, Pusey,' one of the judges said, and what ensued made devotees of regular racing shudder. On each of the anchored skipjacks four men began hauling in the anchor while a team of two pulled heavily on the halyards that raised the huge mainsail. Since the crews worked at uneven speeds, some boats got under way quicker than others, which meant that they were free to cut across the path of the slow starters, impeding them further. But sometimes the early boats miscalculated, and the slow starters generated enough speed to ram their opponents and delay them. When this happened, crews from both boats cursed and threw things and tried to cut rigging.

One of the judges, a gentleman from a Long Island yacht club, said as the big boats slammed into one another, 'This isn't racing. This is marine suicide.' And when Pusey Paxmore said, with some relief, 'We got them off to a good start,' the visitor replied, 'Start? Good God, they're all disqualified.'

The first leg was a long run eastward with the wind directly aft, and Captain Boggs depended upon this to give him an early ad vantage; indeed, it looked as if he might outdistance the field, but the *Eden* and the old *H.M. Willing* from Tilghman lagged only a short distance behind. The latter was a memorable boat; it had been sunk twice, refitted three times: 'Cain't be more than seven percent of the original timbers left. All rebuilt, but she's still the *H.M. Willing*, because it ain't the timbers that determines a boat, it's the spirit.'

'We're in good shape,' Captain Cater assured his crew, 'because in ten minutes we swing onto a starboard run, and then we fly.'

He was right. Halfway to Patamoke the skipjacks had to veer to the southeast, which meant that the strong wind would blow from the starboard quarter, the exact advantage the *Eden* needed. How she leaped forward! Her great boom swung out to port; her bow cut deep; she heeled well over and rode on the chine.

'Stand back, you Black Bastard!' Captain Absalom shouted as his boat passed the *Nelly Benson* and headed for the turn at Patamoke Light.

A real yachtsman who had twice raced to Bermuda watched the turn in frozen amazement; when the *Eden* negotiated it this gentleman said to people near him, 'Why, that man broke six rules! Doesn't anybody say anything?' A waterman who heard the question replied, 'They better not.'

When the turn was completed, it was traditional for the cook to break out a spread and for the first mate to open the portable refrigerators for beer. From here on, the race became a little looser, for emptied beer cans refilled with water began flying through the air, and men with long poles tried drunkenly to impede their competitors.

The food aboard the *Eden* was excellent: ham hocks and lima beans, *krees,* as the watermen pronounced the biting watercress, biscuits and honey with large slabs of yellow cheese. But as each plate was wiped clean, its owner began staring toward the cook's shack, and in due time Amos Turlock appeared with a wide grin, to announce, 'Gentlemen, we got pie-melon pie!' and the crew cheered. When he brought the first pies on deck he said, 'We got lemon on the sour side, vanilla on the sweet, and Sam gets first choice.' He carried two pies, brown-crusted and rich, aft to where the boy watched for mud, and the lad said, 'I takes lemon,' and a large chunk was cut.

A pie-melon was a kind of gourd raised along the edges of cornfields, and when properly peeled and stewed, it produced one of the world's great pies, succulent, tasty, chewy when burned a bit and unusually receptive to other flavors; the proportion was usually three lemon to two vanilla, and today that tradition held, but as the men ate, little Sam shouted, 'Mud! Mud!' and this meant that the centerboard had touched bottom. This did not imperil the skipjack, but if the drag continued, its racing speed would be impeded,

so two men jumped to the pendant of the centerboard and raised it until the lad cried, 'No mud! No mud!' and this meant that the *Eden* was making maximum speed, and that its centerboard rode as deep as practical to ensure adequate protection against lateral drift.

It was now apparent that the race would be decided on the two final tacks, and although the *Nelly Benson* had picked up a slight lead on the port tack, the boats must soon switch to starboard, and there the advantage would move to the *Eden*. 'We're in strong position!' Captain Absalom cried encouragingly, but as he prepared to jibe, Captain Boggs ordered seven of his crewmen aft to launch a barrage of water-filled beer cans at the wheel of the *Eden*, and Captain Cater had to step back to avoid being maimed. In that moment the *Eden* lost headway; the sails flapped; and whatever advantage the Patamoke boat might have gained was dissipated.

But the *Eden* was not powerless. As soon as Absalom regained the wheel, he shipped his skipjack onto a course that would allow its bowsprit to rake the stern of the enemy, and when his tactic became evident the Deal Islanders cursed and threw more beer cans, but Absalom hunkered down, swung his wheel and watched with satisfaction as his long bowsprit swept the *Nelly Benson*, cutting a halyard and forcing the crew to quit their bombardment and try to put together a jury rig that would enable them to finish the race. They did this with such promptness that they entered the final tack only a few yards behind the *Eden* and well ahead of the others.

Captain Boggs now showed why his men called him the Black Bastard. Raising his sails to maximum height, keeping his keel as close to the wind as possible, he started to overtake the *Eden*, and when it appeared that he would succeed, he swung his bow sharply so that the bowsprit could sweep the stern of the Patamoke boat.

'Fend off, back there!' Captain Absalom shouted, but it was too late. The *Nelly Benson* crunched on, her bowsprit raking the *Eden*, and by some hellish luck it banged into a gasoline can carried in accordance with the rule that each boat must be in working dress. The can bumped along the deck, emptying some of its contents before it bounced overboard. The volatile liquid spread rapidly, with one long finger rushing into the galley where Amos Turlock was cleaning up.

A great flame filled the galley and flashed along the deck. Amos, finding himself ablaze, had the presence of mind to run topside and leap into the river. Hugo Pflaum, suspecting that his ancient enemy could not swim, as most watermen could not, grabbed a rope and jumped in after him, and so spontaneous was Pflaum's action that he was able to reach the struggling cook and hold him fast as men on deck pulled the heavy pair back to the *Eden*.

All hands turned to fighting fire, except Captain Absalom, who kept to the wheel, hoping that the starboard tack would allow his boat to pull ahead, but when confusion was at its greatest, the boy aft began to shout, 'Mud!' and Absalom bellowed, 'Man the center-board,' but there was none to hear, so he indicated that the boy should quit his post and try to haul up the dragging board.

A centerboard is a huge affair, often made of oak and a task for two grown men, so the boy accomplished nothing. 'Take the wheel!' Absalom shouted and the boy ran aft to steer the skipjack, while his father ran to the rope attached to the aft end of the centerboard and tugged on it mightily. It rose a few inches and the dragging ceased.

With the fire under control, the Patamoke crew turned to the job of bringing their damaged boat to the finish line. They had lost their lead, but they kept in mind that this was a starboard tack. With burned hands and sooty faces they began to cheer and throw beer cans and trim their sails, but they were impeded by a situation which had never before developed in a skipjack race: the intense heat of the gasoline fire had melted some of the dacron lines into blobs of expensive goo. But Patamoke men were ingenious, and the crew found ways to improvise substitutes and to pass their shortened lines through sheaves and thus keep their boat moving.

It was to be a photo finish, with the *Nelly Benson* slightly ahead, the *Eden* closing vigorously. Crews of the trailing skipjacks began to cheer and big Hugo Pflaum with two of the black crewmen stood forward to repel any new assaults.

'We can make it!' Amos Turlock bellowed, throwing beer cans like mad at Captain Boggs. But the Deal Island men knew how to handle their boat, and while the *Eden* crew was working on their sails they heard the cannon. The race was over and they were forty seconds from the line. The cup, the money, the honor—all were lost. The deck was scarred with flame, their fingers burned with gasoline.

'Damn,' Absalom growled as the *Eden* crossed.

'We almost made it,' his son said.

'Ain't nothin' in the world pays off on near-'ems 'ceptin horse-shoes.'

'It was fun,' the boy said.

'Fun!' his father exploded. 'Goddamnit, we lost!'

That night, when the crews assembled to celebrate and collect their awards, Absalom had the graciousness to approach Captain Boggs, shake his hand and admit, 'You won fair and square.' Those standing nearby cheered and the Deal Islander said modestly, 'God was on our side. Ninety-nine times out of a hunnerd we wouldn't of hit that gasoline can.' And Absalom conceded, 'That's how the dice rolls.'

Mr. Steed, elated by the showing of the *Eden* and pleased to have been accepted into Choptank life so quickly, delivered the final judgment on the race: 'All things considered, we gained a moral victory.'

The Turlocks

THE FACT THAT HUGO PFLAUM SAVED THE LIFE OF AMOS Turlock during the fire aboard the *Eden* did not mean that the stubborn old warden relaxed his determination to capture The Twombly. In semi-retirement, the thick-necked German reported to his office only three mornings a week, but whenever he saw the empty space on his wall of pictures, he resolved anew to find that gun.

His superiors in Annapolis were neither amused nor patient. 'For thirty-nine years you've been telling us, "I'll find that gun any day now." Where in hell is it?'

'We think it's hidden close to where the old marsh used to be. And we know he's using it because on some mornings when he comes to town we can smell powder on his clothes.'

'Sign out a warrant and search his trailer.'

'I been through that trailer four times when he was out. Found nothing.'

It was decided that since Amos used the gun as many as nine or ten times each season, he must keep it hidden somewhere close to the trailer, and Pflaum was directed to hold the place under surveillance, but this raised more difficulties than it solved, for the Turlock establishment had certain extraordinary features. From the enthusiastic potteries in North Carolina, Amos had enlarged his collection of lawn statuary to twenty-one major items, and casual passers-by were usually on hand to admire the art collection. Older people liked the white cement replica of an Italian marble; it showed a naked girl scrunched over from the waist, her hands in position to hide those parts deemed most vulnerable. But children preferred Santa Claus and his eight reindeer.

When Pflaum initiated his regular spying, things were complicated by the fact that Amos had imported an ensemble of eight fairly large pieces which gladdened his heart: Snow White accompanied by seven dwarfs, each carved with maximum cuteness. When trailed across the lawn, the sculptures captivated the public, and the local policeman said approvingly, 'Sort of rounds things out. More grass to trim by hand, but also more fun for ever'body.'

Hugo, seeing the eight additions for the first time, said, 'Place looks even junkier than when it was a shack,' and this was true, for in the old days the cabin, weathered and dilapidated though it was, had shared the dignity of the surrounding woods. But this chrome trailer with its little picket fence and lawn sculptures had been offensive at birth and got worse as it grew older.

What Pflaum particularly disliked was the stiff manner in which Amos had placed the three dwarfs Smiley, Bashful and Grumpy. 'He's got them lined up as if they were soldiers. The others, he at least has them strung out.' He was so offended by the awful aesthetic of this lawn, and so irritated by his failure to find the gun, that one morning he pushed open the low gate guarding the path to the trailer, then jumped back as a hidden spring triggered a set of automobile horns which sounded *Do ye ken John Peel?*

Alerted, Amos Turlock came to the Dutch door and opened the top half. 'Do you like the tune, Hugo? Me bein' a hunter and all that?'

The klaxon greeting had been the last straw, so without extending the amenities Hugo said, 'Amos, I want you to turn in the gun.'

'What gun?'

'The Twombly. I know you have it hidden, and I know you love it. But the time's come, Amos. I want it.'

'I haven't had my hands on that gun—'

'You fired it four nights ago.'

'How would you know?'

'Up and down the river, Turlocks eating geese.'

'We're good hunters, Hugo, all of us.'

'You are good, and you don't need that old cannon any longer.'

'Where could I hide a gun twelve feet long?' With a generous gesture he invited the warden to inspect the trailer, and even shouted, 'Midge, have we got a gun in there?'

'We sure have,' his toothless paramour called back, and forthwith she produced a shotgun. Amos laughed, and Pflaum said, 'I should of let you drown.' Then his irritation got the better of him, and he said, 'Those seven dwarfs look like hell,' and with that judgment he stomped off the premises.

Five nights later, when there was a strong frost in the air and no moon to betray the midnight hunter, Amos summoned Rafe, the grandson in whom he had most confidence. 'We ain't obliged to get ourselves some geese, because we ain't finished the ones we got last time, but a man oughta keep his hand in. We're goin' gunnin'.'

At eleven he and Rafe left the trailer, walked out into the yard, bent down and cautiously pulled on two rings hidden in the grass on which the three dwarfs stood: Smiley, Bashful, Grumpy. Slowly the dwarfs rose in the air, falling backward from a grave twelve feet long. It was a scene from a Dracula movie—even the hinge creaked—except that when the grave was opened, it revealed not a vampire but The Twombly.

With loving care Amos lifted it, stared at the moonless sky and told Rafe, 'Fetch the dog,' and as the Chesapeake bounded out of the trailer, Amos lowered the lid, checked the three dwarfs and led the way through the woods to where the skiffs lay hidden.

It was a perfect night for goose hunting, cold but not blustery, starry but with no moon. When they reached the spot where La Trappe River joined the Choptank they detected large numbers of fowl rafting at the proper distance, and as Amos primed his massive gun and checked the seating of its stock against the bags of pine needles, he whispered to his grandson, 'Best thing a man can do in this world is hunt, or fish, or go arsterin'. God put all these things down here for us to enjoy, but He hid 'em so's only a resolute man can catch 'em. It's our manly duty to try.'

As he sighted along the polished barrel of The Twombly, he saw the glimmer of Orion and he showed the boy how that constellation stalked through the heavens, a mighty hunter seeking game. 'It ain't by chance he comes out in winter. Stands up there to protect us . . . and the gun.' Softly he touched the brass cannon, and then asked, 'How old are you, Rafe?'

'Ten.'

'God A'mighty, boy, this here gun is fifteen times older'n you are. Think of it, fifteen different boys your age coulda' cared for this gun, and now it's your responsibility.'

The red Chesapeake, sensing the geese ahead, was growing restless; Amos hadn't even taken out the short paddles, and the dog feared something might spook those geese. He made soft noises to indicate his displeasure at the sloppy methods being pursued this night, but Amos growled at him to keep silent. He wanted to talk with the boy.

'Man's got only three obligations, really. Feed his fambly. Train his dog. Take care of his gun. You do them jobs properly, you ain't got no worries about such things as mortgages and cancer and the tax collector. You take care of the gun, God takes care of the mortgage.'

'Won't the law . . .'

'The law takes this gun away from us, Rafe, when it's smart enough to find it. I been guardin' this gun for fifty years. You're good for another fifty.'

'But Hugo Pflaum was practically standin' on it that other mornin'.'

'That's why us Turlocks will always have this gun.'

'Why?'

'Because we're smart, all of us, and game wardens is stupid, all of 'em.'

The dog whimpered, eager to get on with the hunt, but he was astonished at what happened. Amos Turlock was climbing gingerly out of the skiff that carried The Twombly and inviting his grandson to take his place with the short paddles.

'Time you learned, son,' he said when the delicate transfer was completed.

'You want me . . .'

'Two things to remember. Aim the skiff, not the gun. And for Christ's merry sake, stay clear of the stock, because it kicks like hell.' With a gentle and loving push he launched the skiff toward the rafted geese, then reached for his dog's head. Pulling the Chesapeake to him, he clutched him nervously as the boy disappeared into the darkness. The dog, sensing that this was an unusual night, stayed close to his master and waited for the great explosion that would project him into the water in search of geese.

It was a long wait, but neither the man nor the dog grew restless; Amos could remember nights when it had taken him an hour of working with short paddles before he had been satisfied with his position, and Rafe had been trained to be meticulous. In the blind, Amos remembered admiringly, Rafe had been the boy with guts to wait.

At last he began to tremble, hoping desperately that his grandson would handle the skiff properly, and the great gun, and the traditions of this river. 'It's a baptism,' he whispered to the tense animal, and the fingers of his right hand twined in the dog's hair so tightly that the Chesapeake whimpered and withdrew, going to his accustomed place in the bow, where he could stand with forefeet on the gunwales, peering into the darkness.

'Blessed God,' the old man prayed, 'let him do it right . . . so he gets the taste.'

Forty minutes passed, and Orion, failing as ever to catch his prey, roamed the heavens. But when the tension in Amos's skiff became intolerable, the night sky exploded, and geese cried, and the dog was gone.

Seven different homes called Hugo Pflaum's office next morning to report illegal gunning on the Choptank. 'I know they were out there, Mr. Pflaum, because two dead geese drifted to my shore. Besides, I was lookin' at the Late-Late Show and remarked to my wife, "That gunfire wasn't on TV." '

The reports were so circumstantial that Pflaum climbed into his pickup and roared out to the Turlock trailer, but as he had anticipated, Amos was absent. Distributing geese up and down the river, he supposed. Midge was gone too, doing her shopping at the Steed store in Sunset Acres. Only a boy, not more than eleven, stood at the corner of the lawn, watching suspiciously as the big, hulking warden moved among the seven dwarfs.

'Who are you, son?'

'Rafe.'

'You can't be Amos's son?'

'Grandson.'

'You wouldn't know where your grandfather is?' No response. 'You wouldn't know where he was last night?' No flicker in the pale-blue eyes.

Hugo was perplexed by the Turlocks, even though his mother and his wife came from that clan; always they seemed stupid, but always in a crisis they mustered just enough brains to outsmart their betters. Look at this boy! Blond hair almost in his eyes, cut in back with the aid of a bowl, vacant stare, heavy woolen pants held up by torn suspenders, didn't even seem to know that Pflaum was a relative of sorts and the game warden. Perhaps, Hugo thought in a misbegotten moment, I can trick this lad.

'Your gran'daddy out huntin' last night?'

'What?' The boy refused to leave his position at the corner of the lawn.

'Does he ever hunt with that big gun?'

'What?'

'Where's he keep it, Rafe?'

'Keep what?' the boy asked, a kind of stupid glaze over his face.

'You tell your father—'

'My father's in Baltimore.'

'I mean your grandfather,' Pflaum snapped.

'Tell him what?' the boy asked.

'That I was here.'

'Who are you?'

'You know damned well who I am. I'm Hugo Pflaum, your uncle more or less. You tell him I was here.'

'I'll tell him. Hugo Pflaum.'

With disgust, the game warden kicked at the sod, gingerly retraced his steps through the garden sculpture and drove back to town.

When he was gone, and well gone, with the pickup far around the bend, Rafe Turlock slumped against the trailer and would have fallen except that he caught hold of a coping. Keeping himself more or less erect, he began to vomit, not once or twice but seven times, until his stomach was empty and his body racked.

Midge found him there, still retching, and thought he might have whooping cough, for the boy would give no explanation for his spasms. She insisted that he go to bed, and he lay there with wet packs on his forehead, waiting for his grandfather's return.

Amos was absent for a long time distributing geese, but when he reached the kitchen and heard the rambling report of his grandson's seizure, he could guess what had caused it. Slipping into the sickroom, he asked, 'Hugo Pflaum here?'

'Yep. He was standin' right on the gun, askin' his questions.'

'About last night?'

'And the gun.'

'And what did you tell him?'

'Nothin', but when he kicked at one of the rings I almost vomited.'

'Midge says you did. All over the place.'

'That was after.'

Amos did not pat his grandson on the head, or congratulate him in any way. The boy had done only what was required, but he did want to let Rafe know that he was pleased, so he whistled for the Chesapeake, and to the dog's surprise, the door was opened and he was invited into the trailer. Quickly he sought out his young master, and realizing that the boy was ill, stayed by his bed, licking his limp fingers.

Amos, closing the door on the room, offered no explanation to

Midge. He walked out onto the lawn to survey his twenty-one sets of sculpture: the deer were lined up behind Santa, the purple flamingo spread its concrete wings toward Sunset Acres, and the seven dwarfs trailed along behind their mistress in seven distinct styles of cuteness. Looking to where the three stood in line, Amos could visualize the great gun nesting at their feet.

'Safe for another fifty years.' he said.

Turlocks survived because they adjusted to their environment. From the moment Amos discovered what those newfangled tape recorders could do, he was satisfied that his goose problems were solved.

He had always been supreme with the goose call, luring birds when others failed, but even at his expert lips that stubby instrument was chancy, and on some days he accomplished nothing. So he drove across the bridge to De Soto Road in Baltimore, where radio shops proliferated, and there bought himself a pair of powerful loudspeakers and a rugged tape recorder built in Sweden.

When he reached home Midge bellowed from the kitchen, 'What in hell you gonna do with that crap?'

His intention was to record the calls of female geese as they came in heat, then to broadcast the calls to hordes of males as they flew overhead. 'We master this machine, Rafe, we'll have enough geese to stock every Turlock kitchen along the Choptank.'

He mastered it so well that hunters from distant counties assembled to observe his miracle. As the wildlife reporter for the *Baltimore Sun* explained: 'Forty minutes before sunrise Amos Turlock and his men move quietly to their blinds and hide themselves beneath pine branches. As dawn approaches and the big geese begin to fly, Amos turns on his Tandberg and through the sky float the sounds of a female goose signaling to the gentlemen aloft. The males, delighted to hear the mating call, wheel in the air and descend swiftly into the muzzles of the Turlock guns.'

Amos enjoyed his monopoly for only one season, then others began to copy it; but it was the legislature that delivered the death-blow. To it came game wardens like the Pflaums, complaining that

the Turlocks were destroying the balance of nature: 'Give them three more years and we'll have the old days back. Not a goose along the Choptank.' The lawmakers, most of them hunters, responded with a tough edict—you can read it in the Maryland Statutes. Turlock's Law they call it: 'No hunter may seduce male geese by means of electronic devices.' And the tape recorders were confiscated.

But a Turlock never quits, and in September of 1977, just before hunting season began, Amos came up with the ultimate stratagem: he rented five cows.

When he fenced them in right beside the creek where geese assembled, he attracted more birds into his field than anyone on the Choptank had ever done before, and Chris Pflaum asked his father, 'What's the old man up to?'

'I don't know,' Hugo said, 'but we better find out.'

Together they drove out to Turlock's spread, and what they saw astounded them. There were the five cows. There were the geese. And on the ground lay more yellow grains of corn than the average outlaw would dare to scatter in four seasons. Whenever Turlock wanted a goose, two hundred would be waiting as they gorged on his illegal corn.

But was it illegal? As Amos explained to the judge, 'All I do is feed my cows extra generous.' By this he meant that he gorged them on whole corn sixteen, eighteen hours a day. His rented cows ate so much that a large percentage passed through their system untouched by stomach acids, and there it lay on the ground, an enticement to geese for miles around.

'I can't find this man guilty,' the judge said. 'He didn't scatter the corn. The cows did.' And when the season ended, with Turlock iceboxes crammed, old Amos returned his rented cows.

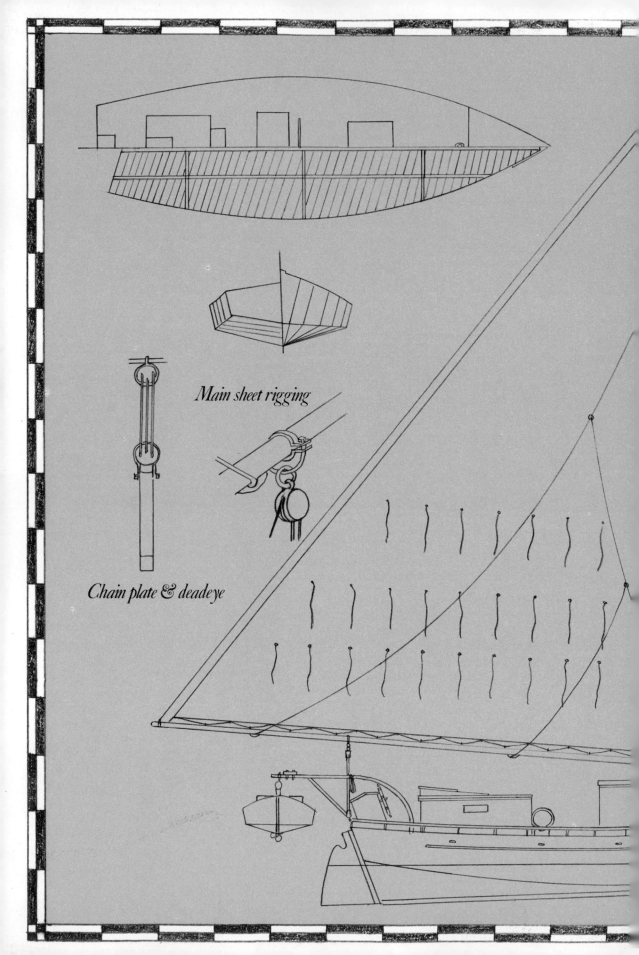

Main sheet rigging

Chain plate & deadeye